PURCHASED FROM
MULTNOMAH COUNTY LIBRARY
TITLE WAVE BOOKSTORE

This special signed edition
is limited to
1000 numbered copies
and 26 lettered copies.

This is copy

The Seven Whistlers

The Seven Whistlers

by

Amber Benson

and

Christopher Golden

SUBTERRANEAN PRESS 2006

The Seven Whistlers © 2006 by Amber Benson and Christopher Golden. All rights reserved.

Dust jacket © 2006 by XXXX. All rights reserved.

First Edition

ISBN
159606-068-9

Subterranean Press
PO Box 190106
Burton, MI 48519

www.subterraneanpress.com

—1—

Rose Kerrigan stood in the sterile, white corridor of the nursing home, her eye drawn to the large corkboard above the nurse's station. She scanned the board while she waited for the day nurse to finish dressing her grandfather. The corners of her mouth turned up in an uncertain grin when she caught sight of a flyer offering the sale of a "slightly used" set of Encyclopedia Britannica.

She couldn't help wondering where one of the *guests* at the Valley Glen Rest Home would put an entire set of encyclopedias. If she went by the size of her grandfather's tiny room, they'd just have to pile the books right on the hospital bed with the patient so there'd be space to walk in and out the door.

The image of her birdlike grandfather sitting up in his hospital bed surrounded by encyclopedias, a confused look on his grizzled face, caused Rose's smile to grow even wider. She knew it was a horrible thought but, as with most horrible or silly thoughts, it just would not leave her brain.

"What are *you* smiling at?"

On the surface, the voice was rich and inviting, its honeyed contralto deceptively lulling. Only with experience could Rose detect the harsh note of condescension. Rose had spent her childhood learning every nuance of that voice because knowledge was power. Knowing what mood corressponded with what tone kept her safe.

There was only one person whose very voice could brew so much tension in her—the voice of Isobel Hartung—the woman Rose called Grandmother.

She turned, forcing a smile, and saw the old woman coming toward her down the corridor, heels clicking on linoleum. Her grandmother wore a neat, camel-colored sweater and linen pants. Her thick gray hair was pulled back in a loose bun that only seemed to highlight the fine bones in her face. She would have been beautiful, if she hadn't been so cold.

"Your grandfather had an episode last night," her grandmother said. "I suppose the nurse has already spoken to you—"

Rose shook her head. No one had mentioned anything to her about her grandfather having an episode the night before.

"Well," Isobel continued, "apparently it was brought on by a minor stroke, nothing that would kill him, but still, I don't want you exciting him this afternoon."

Rose frowned. "I brought the book we've been reading; we're on the last chapter. It usually soothes him. I can't imagine *Huckleberry Finn* upsetting anyone…"

Her grandmother ignored her as if she hadn't spoken at all.

"Just go in and tell him you have other plans for the afternoon. He mustn't be overtaxed, Rose. If you weren't so oblivious, you would see that."

The old woman's words struck her heart like serrated knives. She hated that she let her grandmother affect her so strongly, but this was a cycle that had begun in childhood, something Rose could not seem to overcome.

"But—"

"I have to speak with the doctor then I'll be back to make sure you've gone."

With that, her grandmother turned on her exquisitely-shod taupe-colored heel, and strode off down the hall. Rose watched Isobel's retreating back, her own body sagging slightly as the tension flowed out of her.

God, how the woman makes me want to scream, Rose thought miserably, a migraine starting to eddy around the edges of her consciousness. She slipped the book she had been holding tightly in her hand back into her backpack.

Huckleberry Finn was just going to have to wait for another day.

Ever since her grandfather had moved into the home six months before, Rose had made it her duty to visit him as often as she could. Though the Alzheimer's, which stole his memory, made it difficult for her grandfather to even recognize the faces of his loved ones, Rose did not let it bother her. She just showed up every few days armed with a thick book. If they couldn't share warm family memories, at least, she decided, they would share a good story. Even when old Walt Hartung didn't seem to recognize her, or confused her with his own daughter—Rose's mother—he seemed to take great pleasure in the sound of her voice and her presence.

When Rose entered his room, her grandfather was sitting up in bed, a small frown on his leathered face. Cathy, the day nurse, was putting away the last of his soiled clothes, and gave Rose a wink as she stuffed a pair of dirty socks into a small white laundry bag.

In a low voice meant only for Rose's ears, she whispered, "I heard the witch outside. I was prayin' she wouldn't come in 'til I was long gone!"

Rose nodded wearily.

"Sorry you got the worst of it," she added, catching sight of Rose's pale face and furrowed brow.

"It's all right," Rose answered. "I'm used to it."

"T'aint right," Cathy said, frowning as she pulled the string taut on the laundry bag, and moved toward the door. Again she shook her head, tight blond curls bobbing. "That's no way to treat your own blood."

Rose tended to agree, but let the comment go as Cathy exited, leaving her alone in the Spartan room with her grandfather.

"What's that nurse yammering about?" her grandfather asked, his voice catching in his throat like the air was having trouble escaping his lungs. He was a bit hard of hearing, and was forever asking Rose to talk louder or repeat what someone else had said.

"Nothing, Pappy," Rose said, pulling a chair up to the hospital bed and settling in beside him. He reached out and took her small hand, holding it firmly inside his own weathered one. His skin felt like the papery outer peel of an onion, dry and crackled.

"They'll tell you I was sick last night," he said, his rheumy eyes starting to run a little at the sides. He seemed more agitated than usual, making Rose afraid to answer him. He sensed her misgiving, and scowled.

"Don't listen to a goddamned thing they say, girl. It wasn't sickness that had me last night," he growled. "It was something else. Something far worse than what your own body does to you when you get old."

He clutched at Rose's hand, almost hurting her with his strength. She was surprised by this outburst. It was the most lucid she had seen him in weeks.

"I don't understa—" she began, but he cut her off mid-word.

"There's evil in the world, love. Things your young mind can't grasp, but believe me, they exist, lying in wait..."

"For what?" Rose asked, fear beginning to twist in her stomach.

"For your soul...your *sinner's soul.*"

He squeezed her hand, crushing the tiny, fragile bones that rested inside the flesh.

"Ow! You're hurting me, Pappy," Rose said, her jaw clenching in pain. He seemed to hear her because the pressure on her hand eased a bit, but he still would not let her go.

She stared at him, willing him to return back to normal, but the glazed look in the old man's eyes told her that he was far from okay. She followed his gaze, turning her head to where his eyes were fixed on something just over her shoulder, outside the window. She saw nothing out of the ordinary beyond the glass, just the skeletal brown of leafless trees and the muted gray of the storm-pregnant sky.

"What is it, Pappy?" she said again. "What do you see?"

He let out a low whimper, tears beginning to leak from the corners of his eyes. His face belied the strange memories that seemed to be washing over his brain. This was the kind of lost, delusional gaze she'd had to get used to with him. It broke her heart that she could not draw out from that shell the man he had once been.

"Death's on the hunt for me, Rose," he rasped, fear trembling in his voice. Terror shook him, and in that moment he seemed like a small child, afraid of something in his closet, or the boom of a thunderstorm. He crawled from his bed and tried to hide behind his granddaughter, staring at the window. "They're coming to collect, Rose, for all my sins. Please don't let them have me."

Rose tried to calm him down, to make sense of his delirium. He was frightening her. Still, she couldn't help but feel a bit of joy. It was the first time in over three weeks that her grandfather had called her by her given name.

A sharp claw dug into her shoulder, pulling her up and away from her grandfather.

"What have you done?" Isobel cried, a loose strand of hair falling forward across her flushed face. She pushed Rose into the far wall, not caring that the girl's head slammed painfully against the windowsill.

'I didn't do anything—" Rose began.

Her grandmother fixed her with a glare malevolent enough to stop Rose's protests cold in her throat.

A doctor and two nurses burst into the room behind Isobel. One of the nurses—a tall, dark-skinned man with a wild afro—slipped a sedative filled syringe into her grandfather's arm, pushing the drug into his vein with cool efficiency.

"Go!" Isobel screamed as she pointed a bony finger in Rose's direction.

No one else paid attention to their interaction—the doctor and nurses were still intent upon sedating her grandfather—so they didn't see the hatred that played across the old woman's face, but it chilled Rose to the marrow.

She didn't need any more encouragement—the look was enough. She turned and fled from the room.

—2—

There were no dreams while he slept. The sedatives kept them at bay. His sparse white hair stuck in sweaty clumps to his scalp, his head thrown back haphazardly against a pillow. Long, low snores escaped from the back of his throat, almost waking him. From somewhere in the room came the sound of a chair being pushed backward, its legs squealing against the cold linoleum of the floor, and Walt Hartung awoke with a start.

The old man looked around, unsure of where he was. The room seemed familiar, but he could not place it. Gradually, scraps of memory flowed back, and he remembered this place. Other things came back to him as well, and the fear returned.

He turned his head, saw that he was not alone, and found his fear abated, if only for a little while.

"Bella...?" he said his voice hoarse.

"I'm here, Walter."

She still looks as beautiful as she did on our wedding day, he thought as he stared at Isobel, who sat primly in a nearby chair.

He reached out his hand, and she took it in her own, massaging his fingers. Out of the corner of his eye, he saw the beginnings of a large purple bruise starting to form underneath the skin of his arm. Then he remembered the huge needle, and the grim determination in the male nurse's eyes as he jabbed the syringe into the soft flesh.

"Don't leave me," Walt croaked. "Please stay with me, Bella."

She smiled at him, but her eyes were sad beneath long, mascara-covered lashes. She squeezed his hand again, but did not reply.

"They're coming for me," he whispered, his heart hammering inside his scrawny chest.

A sob escaped him, and great tears began to leak down his face. Helpless to stop them, he turned his face against the pillow, wiping at the tears as best he could. When he looked up at her again, Isobel pulled a tissue from the box on the night table and dabbed at his face, careful not to hurt him. There were no more words.

Finally she leaned forward and brushed her lips against the cool of his forehead. She stayed like that for a moment, breathing in the smell of his skin, then stood and pulled her hand from his, leaving the room.

Rose walked as quickly as she could through the trees, cursing herself for taking the short cut through the cemetery. It was getting darker, and she was usually coward enough to avoid the place during the light of day, so why she had chosen to dare it when the moon was rising like a ripe peach in the sky above her, she had no idea.

She had been on autopilot ever since she'd left the nursing home. The scene she had witnessed there, and the hateful look in her grandmother's eyes, lingered in her mind, and she replayed the incident over and over in her head. The worst part was that she didn't even know what she had done wrong. She hadn't even read from the book. She had simply come in to say hello to Pappy, and then all hell had broken loose.

Deep in her backpack, her cell phone began to buzz, nearly giving her a heart attack. She didn't bother to stop and dig it out because she knew it was only Jenny calling to make sure she remembered they were meeting at The Pennywhistle at six instead of the usual seven o'clock.

It was an age-old ritual—every Tuesday night she and her friends met to share a few pints at the local pub and gossip about the happenings in town. It was a nice way to keep in touch, and to blow off a little steam in the process. Actually, Tuesday was a rule, never to be missed. But the Pennywhistle was sometimes a two or three night a week habit.

Tonight, though, Rose had almost gone back up to her parents' cabin instead of downtown. Her nerves were shot, and her head was a throbbing mess. The idea of brushing down horses, saddling them, carrying bags of feed, and dealing with tourists who'd never been on horseback before made her head hurt even more. But then she remembered that she wasn't on the schedule for tomorrow. She loved working the stables at the Red Oak Inn, but tonight, the idea of a day off tomorrow was bliss.

Plus, her car was parked near her apartment. Whenever she was down in Kingsbury proper, she walked instead of drove. So she had to pass within a few blocks of the Pennywhistle regardless.

Tuesday night. It was a ritual.

So she'd found herself taking the short cut from Valley Glen through the woods—and cemetery—the fastest way to downtown and the warmth of sorely needed friendship. She could not help feeling afraid, but she tried to fight it.

Picking her way through the dead leaves that littered the ground, Rose felt keenly aware of every sound that plucked at the silence of the night. She recognized most of them, could attribute them to the wind and the comings and goings of different animals and night birds. She knew she just needed to keep walking, that the little creatures skittering here and there around her were more terrified of her than she was of them.

She kept telling herself that, keeping her fear at bay.

Then the night filled with a strange, ear-piercing whistle that shook the air around her, and stilled all the other wildlife in the woods.

Rose stopped, frozen in place. She stood rigid, waiting for it to come again, wondering what the hell had made that eerie, shrieking whistle. She'd never heard anything like it before, and she'd walked the wooded mountains around Kingsbury all her life. Now, she heard only silence.

Her body started to relax, only to be jarred by another shriek. She wanted to run, but she couldn't make herself move. She tried to swallow, but found there wasn't a drop of saliva left. Rose could taste the cool of the air around here, and the vast empty space of the woods, which was even now threatening to engulf her.

It began to rain.

Somehow, the cold droplets released her from her fear, and she could move again. She hurried—not quite running—out of the cemetery, and soon the lights of downtown were ahead, and she felt safe enough to begin to feel foolish for her fear.

The old man pulled the covers even further over his head, the transparent whiteness of the sheet barely blocking out the green cast of the fluorescent lights above him. His whole body shook—small tremors making his teeth chatter and his bowels liquefy in his gut. He had known fear before, had stood on the edge of the abyss more than once in his long life, but somehow this was different.

He'd heard the whistle.

Time was no longer on his side.

Outside, the water lashed against the windowpane and thunder bellowed a drum roll for what was about to come. The first shriek had sounded almost ten minutes before, and the second only moments after that.

"Bella...!" He didn't want to be alone now, at the end. He couldn't bear it.

There was another loud burst of thunder and he shuddered, his teeth gnashing together so fiercely that his jaw ached with the effort. In the silence that came after each thunderclap, a new sound pierced the air. The old man screamed, his hands clutching at his bedclothes for the protection they could not provide.

"Go away!" the old man screamed, hysterical now with fear. The shrieking came again, then silence, followed by the sound of something deathly sharp scratching insistently against the glass pane of the window.

19

Dropping the covers, the old man threw himself from the bed. His scrawny legs barely able to hold his weight, he stumbled toward the door.

"Damn you to hell. You won't get me!" the old man screeched, before grasping the doorknob. His breath caught in his throat, and he gasped, unbelieving, as his hands pawed clumsily at the door—which would not open.

From the outside, someone began to bang on the door.

"No..." he said, his voice barely a whisper. He turned, letting his back rest against the doorframe. His gaze was drawn toward the window once more, and Walt Hartung caught sight of what was waiting for him outside. Frail and half-mad, having already lost so much of himself, he knew he could fight no longer.

The only thing left for him to do was die.

His chest tightened with pain and he slid to the floor, down into the embrace of the darkness, and the shrieking of the night.

—3—

The Pennywhistle was already a bustling madhouse when Mike Richards walked in, at a quarter after six. His eyes scanned the room until he spied his friend, Alan Bryce, sitting with his wife, Jenny, at a table in the back corner. The couple were holding hands and gazing into each other's eyes in that moony, giddy, lost way unique to people in love or taking hallucinogens. Mike had never been a huge fan of gooey showings of love, but he figured Alan and Jenny deserved a grace period, as they were still in the thralls of post-honeymoon bliss. They'd only been back from Hawaii for ten days or so.

Jenny caught sight of Mike first, and waved him over to their table. At twenty-five, with her pink Strawberry Shortcake sweatshirt and cut off jeans, she looked ten years younger than she actually was.

"You're late, Richards!" she said as she tucked a long strand of strawberry blonde hair behind her ear and scrunched up her freckle-covered nose.

"But not as late as Rose," Alan added. "It's weird. You're usually our resident space cadet. We figured she'd beat you by hours."

Mike couldn't really argue. He often got so lost in his work handcrafting furniture that time lost seemed to warp around him. But the fact that it was true didn't mean he was going to take shit from Alan.

"You know how it is, Alan. Those of us not completely pussy-whipped don't have to be so worried about our schedules."

A mottled red colored Alan's pale cheeks, and he gave a sheepish grin, flashing his middle finger at Mike. As enjoyable as it was, it really wasn't difficult to make Alan flush. Just tease him, and his Irish heritage betrayed him every time.

Pushing Alan's buttons wasn't hard, but most people wouldn't have dared. Blond and blue-eyed, he stood nearly seven feet tall and so broad he looked as though he'd have to turn sideways to get through most doors. If he ever grew a beard, he'd have been a perfect Viking. Most people were intimidated in Alan's presence, unless they saw him handling the delicate objects for sale in Cat O' Nine Tails, the antique store he owned on Elm Street in downtown Kingbury. Mike had known Alan since grade school and knew the guy was gentle as a lamb as long as you kept his alcohol intake to a minimum.

"Don't poke the bear," Alan warned.

Mike grinned. "Pooh bear, you mean. Oh, bother."

Alan couldn't help it. He laughed. "You're an ass."

"Indeed. I'm gonna grab a beer. You guys need anything? Lovely Jenny? Pooh bear?"

Jenny held up her nearly full glass. "I'm all set, Piglet, but thanks."

"I'm good," Alan said.

Mike headed off for the bar, and returned a few minutes later with a cold black and tan clutched protectively in his hand. He took the seat opposite Alan, lifted his glass in a silent toast to them, and drained the top quarter of his lager-and-Guinness.

"My God, man, go easy on that drink," Alan chided him. "They will make more, you know."

Mike shook his head, and took another sip, then licked the foam off of his upper lip. "All the teasing in the world will not take away the pleasure of this drink."

He'd spent a long, unproductive day in his workshop trying to get the sketches right on the dining room set he was making for Mabel Rutherford. He'd started on the commission almost two weeks before, and he'd hardly made any progress at all in the interim.

That got Jenny talking about her day, and the three of them fell into the relaxed banter of the closest friends. As the conversation went on, Mike found his gaze shifting toward the double doors that marked the entrance to the pub. He kept willing them to open and for Rose to enter, but they stayed firmly shut, thwarting him.

Six thirty came and went, and Mike began to worry that something had happened to her.

"You really think staring like that is gonna make her walk through those doors any faster?" Jenny asked with a sly grin.

Caught, Mike looked away, embarrassed. "No idea what you're talking about."

"Oh, come on!" Jenny chided him. "We're all friends here, Mikey. Might as well be family. Hey, we could be pretty helpful to the cause. But if you're not ready to deal with it, well, then there's nothing we can do to help you…"

The Pennywhistle was a Tuesday night ritual for them. Sure, they all hung out here more than just Tuesday nights. The food and the atmosphere were both perfect comfort. The place had the best Cajun popcorn shrimp known to man, an incredible bread bar, and a selection of beers from around the world. Everything on the menu was excellent, and on weekends they had live entertainment. Mike loved hanging out there, especially with Alan and Jenny. But Rose had been a big part of his motivation ever since their little group had clicked. When Alan and Jenny had first gotten together, and Mike had found out Jenny's best friend was the somber girl who'd hidden behind her dark, curly hair all through junior high, he'd been surprised. But the first time Rose had joined them at the Pennywhistle, the surprise had been even greater. Rose had an effect on him that was nothing short of enchantment.

He shook his head, laughing softly. Jenny was trying to get him to talk about how he felt, but if he ever said anything so ridiculously romantic out loud, Alan would crucify him for all eternity. *Nothing short of enchantment.* He was an idiot. Yet, just because it sounded absurd, that didn't meant it wasn't true. Whenever he saw Rose, she took his breath away.

Jenny knew. She was a perceptive woman, and had wheedled the whole, sad truth out of him one drunken Memorial Day weekend down at Alan's cabin on the Sharpe River. As the last orange of the afternoon had faded into twilight, she had listened to Mike pour out his secret while her giant fiancé snored happily beside her on a deck chair, his head resting in her lap.

Since then she had been teasing him unmercifully, trying to goad him into asking Rose out. Jenny just didn't understand that no matter what she said he was not going to risk losing Rose's friendship by trying to create a relationship when there wasn't one there. If he ever got the feeling Rose had any romantic interest in him at all, maybe that would change. But for now—

As if she'd read his mind, and knew he was pining for her arrival, Rose burst through the double doors, her short black hair wild around her face, brown eyes wide and unfocused. She looked around the room, her brain not seeming to register what she was seeing because she looked right at Mike twice without recognizing him.

"Rose!" he called out, his voice barely loud enough to pierce the wall of sound that filled the pub.

She turned, her eyes finding Mike's face in the crowd, and gave him a shaky smile before pushing her way through the busy pub toward their table. Rose looked windblown and disheveled, and Mike recalled his earlier worry about her lateness with fresh concern. Rose was not one given to slouching on her appearance. She always wore a light dusting of make-up, and kept her short, curly brown hair in check with barrettes.

"I'm sorry I'm late," Rose said breathlessly as she slung her backpack across the back of the empty chair and sat down. Her cheeks were flush with color, and Mike could detect a hint of sweat underneath the fresh citrus bouquet of her perfume.

"No worries," Alan smiled.

"Well, Mike was kinda worried—" Jenny began, a devilish smile playing at the corner of her lips.

He was gonna *kill* Jenny.

"Evil, Mrs. Bryce," he said.

Rose gave them all a strange look, but let it pass. She licked her lips, her brow furrowed slightly.

"Seriously, Rose, I was starting to wonder if everything was okay," he said.

A grateful smile touched her lips, but did not take the distracted worry from her eyes. "I guess I'm okay, now. But the weirdest thing happened on my way over here."

All the amusement left Jenny's face. Mike had seen how stressed out Rose was from the moment she came through the door. Jenny was just getting it now, that this wasn't Rose being flighty.

"What? What's wrong?" Jenny asked.

Rose sighed, already calming down. "I don't know. It sounds really stupid, but on the way over—I walked, even though I was running late—and there was something *out in the woods. I couldn't see it, but it made the most terrifying sound I've ever heard. Like the wind in the trees, but almost...human sounding, too—*"

"Probably a coyote," Alan replied. "I've heard 'em out at night, and it's pretty creepy."

"It wasn't a coyote," Rose said, her voice firm. "It wasn't anything like that. I know what a coyote sounds like, and just about anything else that you might hear in these woods. Whatever it was, it gave me chills I can't even describe. I was too scared to move. I just stood there until it stopped and then I ran as fast as I could."

Mike let his fingers brush against the wool of Rose's sweater. He could still feel the cool of the evening air lingering in the thick fabric.

Alan leaned toward her, over the table, his gaze intense. "It could have been a ghost, Rose. Did you see anything weird?"

Most people would have thought Alan was joking, but they'd all heard him talk about ghosts before. As a child, he claimed to have seen them all the time. It had been ten years or more since the last time. Mike thought Alan had just grown out of a childhood phase, the way some kids did their imaginary friends. But it was obvious that, to Alan, they'd been very real. And he missed them. Jenny had once said that she thought the ghosts were why Alan loved antiques so much—the only way he could still connect to the past—and Mike didn't argue the point.

Rose blinked and stared at him. "I don't...I'm sorry, Alan, but I don't believe in ghosts."

Alan arched an eyebrow and sat back. "Fair enough. If you've got a better explanation for what you heard."

"I'm sure there's a logical—" Mike began, but he was interrupted by the arrival of Dave McKeegan, the Pennywhistle's sole proprietor and bartender. Dave had a shock of gray hair and a round belly from imbibing too much of his own trade. At fifty-something, Dave usually had a twinkle in his Irish eyes, but tonight it was gone.

He put a fatherly hand on Rose's shoulder.

"Rose, honey, there's someone on the phone for you."

Rose gave him a quizzical look.

"I don't—"

Dave shook his head.

"It's important. Why don't you take it in the back room."

Rose stood, her knees nearly buckling under her weight. Jenny was immediately at her side, taking her arm, and helping her toward the back of the pub.

Mike watched as the two women disappeared behind the bar.

"What's going on, Dave?" Mike asked. "What's the phone call?"

The Pennywhistle's owner cast a regretful look toward the back of the pub.

"One of the nurses up at the home. Said Rose told her she was on her way here. Just wanted to let her know..."

"Oh, God," Mike said under his breath.

Dave nodded.

"I expect she's in for a bit of a shock."

Out of the corner of his eye, Mike saw Jenny leading Rose back to the table. Rose's face was ashen, and tears slid slowly down her cheeks.

"He's gone," Rose said, picking up her backpack and slinging it thoughtlessly over her arm. "Heart attack. I shouldn't have let her make me go. He was so scared, and she made it worse..."

Rose trailed off, her face full of bitterness. She didn't need to elaborate. They all knew who she was talking about. Rose's grandmother was known throughout the whole village as a terrible shrew.

With a sigh, Rose glanced around at her friends. When her gaze fell upon Mike, her eyes went wide.

"Mike, your nose—"

He reached up a hand and touched his upper lip. A moment before she'd spoken, Mike had felt the thick wetness there. Now he pulled his fingers away and saw that they were stained red.

"What the hell?" he muttered, grabbing for one of the cloth napkins that lay crumpled on the table.

His nose was bleeding. The copper scent of blood filled his head.

Where had this come from?

"You okay?" Rose asked.

He nodded, holding the napkin against his nose, head back slightly. That was just like Rose. Scared to death in the woods, in tears over her grandfather's death, and asking him if he was okay because he had a stupid bloody nose.

"Just a nose bleed," he said. "It's nothing.

—4—

"Just take it. You'll feel better. I promise."

Rose looked questioningly at the small white and yellow pill that sat squarely in Jenny's hand before reaching out tentatively. It was nearly weightless in her hand. It was odd to her to think something so small was imbued with such power.

She swallowed the pill, chased with a long swig from the glass of apple juice Jenny had poured for her earlier. Though she knew it could not possibly work so quickly, she thought she could feel the pill start to disseminate throughout her body.

As much as she didn't like anyone looking after her, Rose was glad Jenny had insisted on taking her home. Her apartment wasn't very far, but she didn't feel like walking alone. Jenny's rusted blue Mustang had been a welcome sight to Rose parked in the lot behind The Pennywhistle.

"Are you sure you don't want me to stay with you tonight?" she asked, standing in the small kitchen of Rose's apartment.

Rose didn't relish the idea of being alone, but she wasn't going to impose.

"I'm staying at the cabin while my parents are away, remember? I wouldn't even go back up there tonight, but I haven't been back to let Lucy out or fill her bowl since this morning."

Jenny shrugged. "I can sleep at the cabin. I'm rustic."

Rose gave her a sad smile. "That place is hardly rustic. Outside, sure."

"What, you mean you're not roughing it, up there?"

It was a joke between them. They called the place a cabin because it was up a long, woodsy mountain road and from the outside, it had that big old cabin look. But Rose's parents did well for themselves, and inside, the place was practically luxurious, and bigger than it looked.

"I'll be all right," she promised. "Besides, you need to go home to Alan."

Jenny took her hand. "You know I'm only a call away if you need anything."

Rose couldn't help, but smile. Having Jenny for a best friend was a lot like having a second mother.

"Go," Rose said. "I'm fine. I took the pill. Now I've gotta get up to the cabin before I pass out. I'm just gonna curl up in my parents' bed with Lucy and go to sleep."

Jenny sighed, picking up her purse from the counter. "All right. Let's go. I'll walk out with you."

Rose set her juice glass in the sink, shut off the kitchen light, and they left together.

Outside, on the street, Jenny gave her a hug and then climbed into the Mustang, which was parked right in front of Rose's little red Honda. She gave Rose a wave as she started the car and drove away. Rose stood on the sidewalk, shivering a little, looking forward to wrapping herself in one of her mother's Pueblo Indian throws as soon as she got to the cabin. She watched until the Mustang's taillights faded away into the darkness.

Only then did she unlock the Honda and slide behind the wheel. The idea of the big, empty cabin up in the woods would not have been at all appealing if it weren't for the big, gangly, black Labrador she knew would be waiting for her, tail wagging.

As predicted, Lucy practically tackled her when she opened the door. Rose bent down on the threshold and put her arms around the silly, sloppy dog. After a few seconds, she realized that she'd started crying again. Lucy licked salty tears from her cheeks and barked happily.

"Goofball," Rose said.

Lucy ran outside to pee.

"Come right back in," Rose said. "I'll get you some food."

The dog didn't go more than twenty feet from the front door to do her business, watching Rose the entire time, eyes alight with the promise of food.

Rose had been staying at her parents' cabin—if one could call it that with its huge plate glass windows and modern, stark lines—for the last few days ostensibly to look after Lucy, who was really her father's dog. For Rose, it was sort of a vacation from her apartment. Downtown Kingsbury was alive with music and art and the bustle of tourists, but sometimes she liked the quiet of the woods.

It hadn't been hard for her parents to entice her into house sitting. They knew how much she loved the house, and Lucy.

All they had to do was call and ask, and Rose was there in a heartbeat.

Now, she wondered what would happen. Her father had nearly three more weeks of scheduled speaking engagements in the U.K. and Ireland. But Pappy—her mother's father—was dead. They'd have to come home, now. Tonight, she didn't mind the thought of leaving the cabin behind. As small as her apartment was, the big house on the mountain trail made her feel even lonelier.

Lucy trotted back through the door, and Rose closed and locked it, again absurdly grateful for the dog's presence. Still, she felt more isolated than she ever had before.

It's lonely out here in the woods, even with goofy Lucy for company, she mused as she began the walk through the four-bedroom house, securing all the windows and doors and extinguishing any forgotten lights. She stripped off her clothes and took a long shower, then pulled on a tank top and boxers, the pill Jenny had given her working its magic, lulling her grief and anxiety enough that she felt she could actually sleep.

In her parents' master bedroom suite, she found that Lucy had made herself at home. The dog's shiny black coat glowed in the lamplight where she was sprawled on the linen duvet that covered the king-size bed. It was such a silly picture that it made Rose giggle.

Lucy lifted her head and gazed lazily at her.

"Goofball," Rose said, crawling onto the bed with Lucy. The big dog rolled over, letting her huge body press against Rose.

"Stop it!" Rose giggled, pushing the big dog back over onto the other side of the bed. "You're hogging the bed, dummy."

Lucy raised an eyebrow, her long pink tongue stretching out from the side of her mouth, trying to lick Rose's arm.

"No! Not the dreaded dog slobber," Rose groaned, but it was too late. Lucy was already slopping buckets of dog drool onto Rose's arm. Instead of pushing Lucy away this time, Rose began to pet the big dog, rubbing and scratching at the sweet spots behind Lucy's ears.

Cold night air slid through the open window, encircling Rose as she slept. Lucy whimpered in her sleep, her legs kicking back and forth as she ran after some imaginary creature in her dreams.

It came without warning, a shrill high-pitched cry that woke the dog and set her to barking.

Rose stirred. "What is it, Lucy?"

Her eyes were still caked in sleep and her body was not fully under her control as she sat up and put a reassuring arm on the dog's flank. Another cry tore through the night air, the same reedy whistling sound Rose had heard in the woods just after nightfall.

"Oh God," she whispered, turning to stare at the open window.

For an instant she froze, but then she slid out of bed and shut the window, slamming it hard in its casing. Lucy jumped down from the mattress and came to stand by Rose, a low growl simmering in her throat. Rose instinctively reached down, clutching the fur at the back of Lucy's neck for comfort.

"It's okay, girl."

But the dog was not soothed. She erupted into a barking frenzy as another whistling shriek tore through the night. Lucy slipped out of Rose's grasp and darted out of the bedroom, barking wildly.

"Lucy, get back here!"

Rose followed the dog down the hall and into the living room, where Lucy stood barking at the French doors that led to the deck and the back yard, and the woods beyond. As Rose reached for her, the dog bounded away again, bulleting from living room to kitchen.

The dog flap in the kitchen door had been installed years ago, when her parents had a terrier. It only swung outward, so forest animals couldn't use it to get inside. Lucy had never even tried to use it before, given her size, but as Rose chased her into the kitchen, she saw the Lab forcing herself through the too-small rectangle, rear legs scrabbling for purchase on the tile floor.

"Lucy, Jesus, what the hell are you doing?" she screamed, afraid that the dog would hurt herself.

But then the Lab popped out through the doggie door and the flap closed behind her, leaving Rose gaping stupidly at the place she'd been a moment before.

"Damn it!" Rose snapped. She didn't want to go outside. But Lucy wasn't giving her a choice. With trembling hands, she unlocked the kitchen door and stepped outside.

The wind whipped at her slender form, the tank top and boxer shorts she'd worn to bed little protection against the cold. She shivered as her bare feet found purchase on the dew-soaked redwood decking, the chill of the air pervading not just her skin, but her bones, as well.

"Lucy!" she shouted, her voice carried back at her by the wind. She scanned the woods behind her parent's house, but could see no sign of the dog.

Then she heard angry barking coming from the nighttime shadows on her left. She turned to find Lucy standing at the edge of the backyard, her teeth bared, low growls and yips erupting from her lowered muzzle.

"Lucy!"

Rose ran across the deck and down the stairs, but Lucy ignored her, still barking at something further out in the woods. In a dozen strides she was at the dog's side, and she knelt down and took hold of the scruff of Lucy's neck.

"Come on, you stupid, crazy dog!" Rose said, trying to drag her back into the house. But Lucy wouldn't budge. She continued to bark and strain against Rose's hold.

There was a thrashing sound amongst the trees, and Rose took a step backward, staring into the darkness. Maybe Lucy wasn't stupid after all. Maybe the stupid one was whoever would follow her out into the yard at night when that shrieking whistle filled the air.

Alan thought it was ghosts. What if he was right? Hell, what if it was something worse?

Fear raced through her and Rose scanned the trees. Something moved, and she couldn't breathe. But then her gaze locked on it, the thing that Lucy had been barking at, and she could only stare in wonder. A beautiful silver stag stood less than a hundred yards from her, antlers gleaming in the moonlight. It flipped back its ears, listening to something, and then it turned and looked straight into Rose's eyes.

'Oh…" she said, more an exhalation than a word. She had never seen anything so beautiful in all her life. She wanted to let go of Lucy and walk over to the stag, perhaps even touch it, but she knew it would bolt long before she could close the gap between them.

Entranced as she was, Rose almost didn't hear the shrill whistling cries that began to fill the air. A twin voice seemed to have joined the first, two shrieks echoing in the dark, playing call and answer somewhere deep in the woods.

"Let's go, Lucy," Rose said, pulling the whining dog by the scruff of her neck. She wished she had the leash to slip into the ring on the dog's collar so she could have more control.

"Lucy! Come on!"

The dog stood frozen, her whole body stiff, not allowing Rose any give at all.

The whistling cries came again, much closer than before. Close enough that Rose whipped her head up and searched the trees again. Lucy began to bark madly, slobber spraying the grass. The stag hunched a moment, as though it sensed the approach of whatever owned those cries, and then it took off, long forelegs bounding through the brush.

It had gone only a few yards before something huge and dark leaped out of the shadows and dragged the stag down with its claws. Huge jaws closed on the stag's flank. The beast was silent as it started to pull the stag into the underbrush. A second one shot out of the trees and joined the kill, stilling the beautiful stag's twitching hind legs.

Rose covered her mouth with her hand to stop the scream that was building behind her lips. She yanked Lucy back with all her might, half-dragging, half-carrying the black lab back toward the house. The sounds of slaughter that came from the darkness of the woods made her stomach lurch with disgust. But the fear was far worse. The stag had been beautiful, but if it had not been there, those things might have come for Lucy...or for Rose herself.

Her insides felt hollow and cold. When they reached the deck, Lucy at last began to cooperate, and Rose rushed the dog through the kitchen door, slamming it behind them. She locked it, threw the bolt, and put the chain across as well, then she staggered back against the stainless steel island that stood in the center of the kitchen and slid down into a crouch on the floor. She couldn't stop shaking, even when Lucy nuzzled against her, the dog's warmth like an electric blanket.

—5—

The sun was barely above the horizon when Jimmy Lizotte made his first cast of the day. Nothing in the world gave him as much peace as fishing on the lake. He'd get up at five o'clock, walk down to the dock with a cup of coffee and a bag of the little cinnamon donuts Hannah always bought him at the Buffalo Nickel General Store, start up the outboard and have the little boat out on the water before he'd even taken a piss. That early in the morning, he could whip it out and piss right over the side and nobody was there to see it.

Now he sat there on the cushion he'd bought over the summer. The air was cool and the water dark this early. There weren't any bugs out yet. His line disappeared into the smooth surface of the lake.

Fuckin' bliss.

Jimmy took a sip from his coffee, congratulating himself on how smart he'd been to buy Hannah the machine last Christmas. He could prepare it the night before, set the timer, and wake up to the smell, like his life was a tv commercial. No calls for this electrician on weekends. Weekdays, he tried not to schedule anything before eleven o'clock, so he could get in a few hours on the lake. Half the time he didn't catch anything the law would have let him keep, and even when he did, it was barely enough for dinner, but that wasn't the point.

It was called fishing, not catching.

It's about the Zen, he told Hannah on a regular basis. She never got it, but that was all right. Most days she loved him enough to understand he just needed it, the way some guys needed beer. And fishing didn't do to a marriage what too much booze or too many nights in the titty bars would do. Hannah didn't mind. Most days. And on the days when she did, Jimmy didn't much care…once he was out on the lake, what was she going to do? Skip stones at him?

He took a deep breath and let it out. The pine trees at the lake shore were silhouetted by the rising sun. The chicory coffee was warm and sweet. Jimmy set the cup down and slid his hand into the plastic bag to retrieve a cinnamon donut. God's perfect food, as far as Jimmy was concerned.

A breeze rippled the surface of the lake and made him shudder a little. It felt good, though. He took another sip of coffee to offset the chill. The breeze came again, but this time, it carried a strange sound.

Jimmy frowned. "What the hell is that?" he whispered to himself.

The whistling noise struck him oddly enough that he disturbed his comfortable position, sitting up and looking around, trying to determine where it was coming from. It wasn't any ordinary whistle, not some bird call or policeman's warning. When he was a little boy he'd often heard the whistle that sounded the beginning and end of the work day at the lumber mill across the lake, but the mill had been closed twenty-three years, and this wasn't the same sound anyway. It reminded him more of the sound falling bombs always made in Bugs Bunny cartoons, but even then, there was more to it. The noise seemed a combination of sounds to him; a distant, reedy whistle, and a scream.

Then, as abruptly as it had begun, it ceased.

Jimmy kept looking around, fishing rod in one hand, brows knitted in unsettled curiosity. He told himself it was some kind of bird, though he'd been fishing on Goodman's Lake all his life and never heard anything like it. Some migratory breed, he figured. Global climate change had driven it north. Or east. Or something.

But as he settled down again, movement in the shadows of the pines drew his gaze. On the end of the dock where he kept his boat sat an enormous black dog. At this distance, it was hard to say for sure, but the dog seemed to be looking at him. Staring. The massive hound must have been wild, because he didn't see an owner anywhere. He wondered if it might be a wolf. This beast was way too big to be a coyote.

It just sat there, unmoving. It didn't scratch itself or wag its tail. The dog sat remarkably still, watching.

The tug on his line startled him enough that he nearly dropped his fishing rod, and he twisted around so quickly that his coffee sloshed onto his shirt. He cursed loudly and set the cup down, grateful that it wasn't hot anymore. At the same time, he jerked the rod back, setting the hook, and started to reel. He wound in a few feet of line and then let the fish rest a second. It darted back and forth, struggling to free itself from his hook.

"Come on, baby. Come to Jimmy," he said under his breath as he started to reel again. It felt big enough to be a keeper. Maybe big enough to feed both him and Hannah at dinner tonight.

41

There were a lot of things Jimmy Lizotte loved about his wife, but near the top of the list was that she never got tired of eating fish. Girl knew a thousand ways to cook the catch of the day.

The rod arced down toward the water like a dowsing rod. Jimmy grinned widely and kept reeling. Something silver flashed beneath the dark surface of the lake, and as he wound in a few more inches of line he saw the fish fighting him. It had to be a two-footer.

"Come on, beauty."

The fish was heavy and strong. It gave a massive tug, one last-ditch effort to escape him, and Jimmy rocked on his cushion, the boat tipping a little. He laughed and looked down into the water, and then a frown creased his forehead.

There were other silver flashes down there, some small and some as big as his catch. Fish knifed through the water around the boat. At first he saw only a few, but quickly they multiplied into dozens. A long dark shape darted toward the fish on his hook, and the line swayed to one side.

"You've gotta be shitting me," Jimmy said, chuckling in disbelief.

The swarm of fish—he couldn't really call them a school since they were all different sizes and types—gathered around the one on the hook, swimming right into it, bumping the catch and the line both. Jimmy tried to reel, but felt another powerful tug in downward. The rod bent further toward the water.

This was the craziest thing he'd ever seen. It was as though the fish were trying to save the one on his hook.

He stared down into the water. The sun rose above the trees and its light shone across the lake. In that same moment, he saw the blood clouding the water below him, and little bits of floating flesh.

The fish weren't trying to save his catch. They were eating it, like sharks in a feeding frenzy.

"No fuckin' way," he whispered.

But at least one of them was still on his hook, still tugging down. Jimmy tried to fight it, but the fish were strong, and the whole thing freaked him out. He took his knife from the sheath in his tackle box and cut the line. It had been pulled so taut that when it let go, he fell backward, and accidentally sliced the knife across the ball of his right hand.

He swore loudly, furiously, and let go of the rod. It banged on the side of the boat as it fell overboard and instantly sank into the darkness. Jimmy screamed in frustration and pain, wadding up a fistful of his sweatshirt and pressing it against the cut. The sting of that slice ran up his arm, but it hurt even less than the loss of the rod and reel he'd never see again. The cut could be stitched. His rig was money he could never get back.

Something bumped the boat. Not hard enough to rock it, really. It was more of a slap. But then it came again, and again, and then it was as though all of those fish were pelting themselves against the boat from beneath.

When he knelt to start the outboard, he crushed his cinnamon donuts beneath his knees. He hung his head and laughed at the absurdity of it all. He had to use his left hand to start the motor, and for a moment he was sure it wasn't going to start. This day had been one piece of bad luck after another, and it only made sense he'd have to swim back to the dock. But then the motor roared to life. A bunch of fish swam at the propeller and there was a grinding noise as the motor worked overtime, hacking them to chum.

43

He pointed the prow toward the dock, and headed in, wondering how the day had gone so completely wrong. His Italian grandmother had always talked about the Malocchio, the evil eye, and it sure as hell felt like someone had hit him with that whammy. But it wasn't the bad luck that made him feel like he had spiders crawling under his skin, and it wasn't the stinging pain from the slice on his palm. It was the behavior of those fish. That had been damned unnatural. Just plain wrong, and weird.

It scared him a little.

Hannah Lizotte woke to the smell of smoke. She called out for Jimmy even as she leaped from bed and threw her robe on. As she ran down the stairs, she lost her footing and tripped. Catching herself on the handrail, she twisted her wrist, hissing in pain as tendons tore. Hannah cradled her wrist against her chest as she ran into the kitchen and saw the coffee machine engulfed in flames, the black plastic melting and running down over the kitchen counter. The fire had started to spread on the counter.

Terror raced through her. There were too many things in this house that she could not bear to lose. Fire had always been her biggest fear. A flash of fury went through her as she mentally blamed her husband, thinking Jimmy had somehow left the machine on, though she knew it could have been an electrical fire.

Wincing with the pain in her wrist, she ran to the sink, choking on black, stinking smoke, and turned on the faucet. They had a spray attachment on the sink that was more powerful than the shower head in their bathroom. She switched it on, and began to hose down the burning coffee machine.

A fleck of burning black plastic splashed up at her and stuck to her cheek, burning, searing into her flesh. Hannah screamed, wiping at her face, trying to get it off, but it was stuck. She managed to keep the water spraying on the coffee maker until the flames were doused.

Only then did she let herself sink to the floor, tears and a trickle of blood running down her face.

Half a mile from the Lizottes' house, a sudden gust of wind blew down a dead, towering pine tree. It crashed down on Ray Winston's house, totaling the brand new Saturn he'd given himself as a fortieth birthday present.

On Charles Street, the brakes gave way on the mail truck and Audrey Tosches panicked. Before she could get control of the vehicle, she was up on the sidewalk and careening through the plate glass window that fronted Kelley's bar. She wept as she considered the irony of a twelve-stepper crashing her postal truck into a bar. Then the jagged remaining portion of the plate glass window fell like a guillotine and shattered her windshield. The steering wheel stopped the plate glass before it would have reached her legs, but she'd had her hands at ten and two like they'd taught her at driver's ed when she was sixteen, and three fingers on her left hand were severed.

The blood scared her more than the pain.

Seventy seven year old Aaron Chomsky caught his slipper on the metal lip that separated the linoleum of his kitchen floor from the bare wood of his basement stairs. For an old man, he was pretty spry, and he reached out to grab the doorknob.

It came off in his hand, and he fell.

At the Red Oak Inn, the refrigerator had died overnight, spoiling all of the food that Jenny would have made for guests at dinner that evening.

When Alan arrived at his antique shop, Cat O' Nine Tails, the heat was running and there was an oddly metallic, moldy smell coming from the vents. When he went downstairs, he found that the boiler had given out, and water had soaked through the bottoms of dozens of cardboard boxes, perhaps damaging many of the items he had in storage.

Sheer bad luck. The boiler had been two days past its warranty.

Upstairs, he kept the door open to let the smell out. A strange whistling noise filled the street and he went out onto the sidewalk, searching for its source. A few seconds later, it stopped, and he shrugged and turned to go back inside.

On the street corner there stood the biggest black dog he had ever seen. It stared at him. Though it did not growl or bare its teeth or even take a step nearer, Alan felt waves of menace coming off of the dog.

He closed the door, and went about opening windows instead.

—6—

Rose woke with a gasp, as though she'd stopped breathing in her sleep and only panic had brought her awake. Eyes open wide, she drew several long breaths and her heartbeat slowed almost to normal. Her head felt stuffed full of cotton, almost as though she was hung over, but she hadn't been drunk last night.

An image flashed across her mind like the fragment of a dark dream—the silver stag, so breathtakingly beautiful, completely ethereal—dragged down by massive, slavering black hounds. She squeezed her eyes together as though that might make the image go away, and was surprised when she was at least partially successful. Still, it lingered just below the surface of her thoughts like the echo of a nightmare.

A knock came on the door. Recognition sparked in her, and she felt sure that this was not the first knock, that the sound had been what had actually roused her. Certainly it was not that she was ready to wake up. She still felt exhausted, dull-witted, and heavy, but she forced herself up out of bed.

In boxers and tank top, she padded across the floor of the cabin.

"Who is it?" she called.

"Rose. Open the door."

Grandmother. As always, so impatient and imperious she would not even identify herself. Like Rose should have been able to see through the damned door and prepared a banquet for her arrival, with trumpeters and a red carpet strewn with flowers.

Be kind. Her husband's just died.

So why did Rose feel that Pappy's death hurt her far more than it did her grandmother? Hard-nosed as she was, the woman had loved him. Rose was sure of that. Pappy was the only one her grandmother had ever seemed to love, and even then the emotion had never shown in her face or in physical affection, only in the way she had listened when he spoke, and kept close to him wherever they went.

For his sake, be kind, Rose thought.

With a sigh, her heart a tight fist of grief over her grandfather's passing, she unlocked the door and pulled it open.

The old woman had tired eyes, pinched at the corners with what might have been sorrow. Her jaw was rigid as ever, chin high. She wore a black skirt and a cream colored blouse beneath a black sweater, and looked more than a little like a nun. The grieving widow. These were mourning clothes. Her grandmother had always been a stickler for traditions.

"Good morning, Grandmother," she said, stepping aside. "I guess I overslept. Can I make you a cup of tea?"

"Don't trouble yourself on my account," the old woman said, brushing past Rose as she entered the cabin. "I've just been making funeral arrangements for your grandfather and thought you'd like to know what I've planned."

Rose shut the door. Her grandmother strode across the living room into the quaint, country kitchen. She sat in one of the two chairs at the small, round, rustic table and clasped her hands in front of her. Rose went past her, filled the teakettle, and switched on the burner.

The old woman would never ask for anything, but she'd want the tea—would be insulted if Rose didn't serve her something.

"It's thoughtful of you to come," Rose said.

Her grandmother sniffed as though it had been an insult.

Rose reached up into the cabinet for a pair of teacups and reluctantly fetched saucers as well. Tradition, after all. Her hands shook a little and a little twist of nausea hit her. She really did feel hung over. Her face felt slack and she looked at her funhouse-mirror reflection in the tea kettle—she was pale, dark crescents beneath her eyes.

"I spoke to your mother this morning," her grandmother said. "She and your father will be coming home for the funeral, of course. But it will be several days before they return, and I can't wait for them to have the wake. Even so, I think it's hideous when people have days of a wake, two sessions a day, like it's a Broadway play and they need a matinee."

Her upper lip curled back with repugnance.

Rose took teabags out of the cabinet and dropped one in each cup. She turned to face her grandmother. "People have hectic lives. Providing different times for them to pay their last respects makes it easier for them."

"Why should it be easy for them?" the old woman asked, genuinely mystified. "My husband...your grandfather is dead, Rose. If the timing of his passing isn't convenient for people, to hell with them."

Her voice had gone a bit shrill on the word *dead*. Rare proof of her love for the man.

"We'll have one wake. Friday night. And on Saturday morning, we'll have a funeral mass. Father Cahill is young. I wish Father Hughes still ruled the roost at St. Margaret's, but there's nothing to be done for it. Still, I've told our young priest that I won't stand for any short cuts. It's a full funeral mass, not some benediction and then a burial. If we don't do the entire mass, we might as well bury him in the yard next to the piss-happy dog your mother doted on as a girl."

Rose felt her mouth hanging open, but couldn't force herself to close it. Her grandmother had always been an opinionated woman, but she'd never been so crass. Quiet and stern, quick with a judgment, yes. But this brutal frankness was a surprise, even from her.

"Oh, close your mouth, Rose. You'll catch flies."

She did as she was told.

"You look like hell, by the way," the woman said, sitting so primly in her cane chair, haloed by the morning sunshine coming through the kitchen window.

"Oh, thank you," Rose replied, giving a supermodel turn as though to show off the latest fashion. "It's a new look I've been cultivating. Glad you noticed."

Then she faltered, dizziness weakening her, and had to catch herself on the edge of the counter.

"Rose?" her grandmother said, her tone more accusation than concern. "Are you all right?"

With a scowl of disgust, she clenched her teeth and turned her back on the old woman. To keep from saying something she'd regret, she busied herself with the tea, though the kettle had not yet whistled. She made her grandmother's just as she liked it, with a single dollop of milk, and then carried cups and saucers to the table. Still silent, she went back for spoons.

Her grandmother was dipping her tea bag as though fishing for something, but her eyes were locked on Rose.

"What is it?" she asked, and if Rose had been the type to fool herself, she might just have been able to imagine she heard actual concern in her grandmother's voice.

Instead, Rose laughed softly, darkly.

"You know, I'm sorry if I show my emotions more than you do. I know you probably think it's obscene or something, but I hurt, inside. I'm screaming, inside. All my life, Pappy was the only one I ever thought really saw *me* when he looked at me, instead of what he wanted me to be. He talked to me about what was in my heart, not what he thought should be there. Now you're going to tell me that he was your husband, and no one can miss him more than you do, no one can grieve as much as you. And maybe you're right. But I can't hold it inside like you! I think about never hearing his voice again, and I just can't—"

Her voice broke. Hot tears ran down her cheeks. She shook her head in frustration and turned away, wiping her eyes. All she wished for at that moment was someone who truly loved and understood her to be there and just hold her while she cried out the pain in her heart, but the only one who'd ever really fit that description was the one she was crying for. Her grandmother would not embrace her. Rose would never have expected it.

A chill went through her and she shivered.

"I know you loved him," her grandmother said. "And he loved you."

Rose shook her head again, at a loss. "But you don't understand why I look like hell?"

The old woman picked up her teacup in her right hand, and the saucer in her left. Daintily, she sipped her tea, just as she'd been taught by her mother when she was a tiny girl.

Lucy, finally roused from her doggy slumber, ambled out of the bedroom and into the kitchen. She made several circles and then plopped down on the floor.

With a sigh, Rose slumped in her chair. The sight of Lucy had brought back the terror she'd felt last night, and her revulsion at the sight of those hounds tearing into the stag. Another twist of nausea hit her, and she took a sip of tea to try to settle it down. She rubbed her eyes and took a deep breath, trying to cleanse the memory.

"Is something else troubling you?" her grandmother asked, taking another sip of tea.

Rose glanced away a moment, then met her gaze. "Bad as yesterday was, last night only made it worse. I had a little scare outside. More than a little, really. I've never been so scared."

Her grandmother knitted her brows. "What do you mean, scare?"

"Lucy went a little crazy during the night, barking like a nut. She ran out into the back yard and in the woods I saw this deer. A stag. The most beautiful animal I've ever seen. It was huge, twelve points at least, but in the moonlight it looked almost silver. It took my breath away."

Rose cringed at the memory, which rose again as she spoke of it.

"It was standing there, and then it bolted. I don't know if it heard them coming, or smelled them, but it started to take off the way animals do when there's fire coming, or something meaner than them on the hunt. Two black dogs came out of the trees, so dark they could have walked right up to me and I wouldn't have seen them until the last second. They were huge, bigger than any dog I've ever even heard of, and wild. The dogs attacked the stag, dragged it down, and just tore it apart right there."

The teacup tumbled from her grandmother's fingers. Tea splashed as it struck the edge of the table, breaking off the china handle. Then it hit the ground and shattered into gleaming shards in a spattered puddle of tea."The Whistlers," her grandmother rasped, her gaze distant, the china saucer still held firmly in her left hand.

"What? Grandmother, what? Are you okay?"

The old woman blinked and looked down at the mess she'd made. "Oh, my goodness. I'm so sorry, Rose. Your mother loves this china set."

Rose got up and fetched the dustpan and brush from under the sink and set about sweeping up the shards.

"Don't worry about it, grandmother. What about you? Are you all right? You looked like you'd just kind of gone away for a minute there. I thought you were having a stroke or something."

Regaining her composure as Rose got a dishcloth to wipe up the spilled tea, the old woman waved such concerns away.

"I'm fine. It's a stressful time, that's all. And what a horrible nightmare for you to have."

Rose blinked and stared at her. "It wasn't a nightmare. I saw it happen, right outside. Lucy was with me."

"You must be confused, dear," the old woman said. "Grief and exhaustion will do that. It must have been a dream. Just a nightmare, Rose."

Pretty vivid for a nightmare, she thought. But she said nothing, just finished cleaning up the mess. There was no point ever in arguing with her grandmother. Time to change the subject.

"You're sure you're all right?" Rose asked.

"Perfectly."

"What was that you said before? When you were zoning, you said something. Whistlers?"

"I don't know what you mean, dear," her grandmother said. "Now, about the funeral. I'd like you to do a reading at the mass. I've got it all picked out. And if you don't have anything appropriate to wear to the wake and the funeral, please tell me, and I'll take you shopping to pick something out."

Rose stared at her. "I have that black dress I wore to your anniversary party a few years ago. I'm sure it still fits."

"Good. Good." Her grandmother stood, smiled thinly, and started for the door. "I'm off, then. I have to bring a suit to the funeral home for them to dress your grandfather. He'd want the red tie, I think. Something dashing."

"That'll be nice," Rose said, though she was barely aware she was speaking. The conversation had been surreal. She drifted across the cabin and stood by the door, seeing her grandmother out.

The old woman climbed into her car, waved once, and drove away.

Rose didn't remember her grandmother ever calling her "dear," before. Now she'd done it twice in as many minutes. Yet there was nothing intimate about it. She'd seemed distracted, almost nervous.

Dear.

Weird.

—7—

The Red Oak Inn was quiet. The breakfast room was almost empty and the tables were slowly being bussed. Rose went through the room and into the kitchen, where she found Jenny scraping the grill and cleaning up her workspace. Jenny was the best chef the inn had ever had. Everyone said so, and Rose didn't doubt it.

"Hey."

Jenny turned around, a soft look of sympathy on her face. "Hey. Don't tell me you're working today."

"No. I just thought I should come in and talk to Max in person. I'm scheduled for tomorrow. I can work that shift. But the wake's on Friday and the funeral Saturday, so—"

"He'll be fine. I spoke to him already, and I talked to Cheyenne as well. She's going to take whatever shifts you need. I explained how close you were to him."

She didn't have to say who *him* was.

The Red Oak Inn sat on the mountainside just outside of town, with a perfect view of the picturesque little New England village spread out below. The church steeple and the pond at the town center and the old-fashioned railroad that ran right through downtown were like a postcard, viewed from the front windows of the inn. But it was the best of both worlds. The touristy village was a few minutes' drive, but the inn fronted more than a hundred acres of wooded hills that was part of their property, and there were horse trails all through it.

Rose had worked with the horses for three years, and loved them all. Cheyenne was the horse trainer, and the boss when it came to the stables. But Rose had learned a lot from her about how to care for them, and how to deal with the inn's guests who paid to ride the trails.

"You going to go and see Trouble?" Jenny asked.

Despite her sadness, Rose smiled. Trouble was her favorite of the horses; a persnickety mare with a love of Granny Smith apples that knew no bounds. The temptation to go and see her, brush her down, the peace that would bring was a strong lure. But the image of those dogs tearing at the stag last night still lurked in her mind.

Jenny wiped her hands on her apron and came over to Rose.

"You need anything?"

Rose nodded. "A shotgun and a good shrink."

"What?" Jenny said, a dark look crossing her features.

"No, no, the shotgun's not for me. I loved Pappy, but I'm not in a hurry to join him. Just, something weird happened last night, and I can't get it out of my head."

For the second time that morning, she recounted the terrible, bloody scene from the night before.

"My grandmother thinks it was a dream," Rose said with a short, humorless laugh. "It wasn't any dream. She got all freaky when I talked about the dogs, though. Kind of spaced and dropped her teacup, and she said something about whistling. I thought she was having an aneurysm or something. I'm still not sure she didn't."

Jenny was nodding even before she finished. "Yeah, yeah. The Seven Whistlers. I've heard that one."

Rose cocked her head. "What one?"

"It's a story. A legend. Giant, black dogs. Hellhounds or something. They bring bad luck, I guess. I mean, obviously it's just a story. But you know how your grandmother is about traditions and stuff—"

"Yeah, but not superstitious traditions. At least, not that I ever knew."

Jenny shrugged. "I'm just saying, that's what your story reminded me of, too. Maybe it freaked her out. Old people can get like that. And with your grandfather just passing…"

She let the words trail off and shrugged again.

"I guess. But how come I don't know the story and you do? I've never heard that legend before."

"It's an old thing. Celtic, maybe. I don't know. I'm sure I only know it from my Aunt Arlene. You know how she is with all the folklore and stuff. With her painting and her whole earth-mother thing, she's the town oddball. But she loves all that stuff, knows all the folklore, local and otherwise. It's her hobby."

"I thought painting was her hobby."

Jenny shook her head. "You'd think, right? But no, she makes a living painting. I told you she sells some of her paintings as book covers."

"Guess I never thought much about it. Never took her all that seriously."

"Nobody does. It's her charm. She seems so dippy, but she's serious about her passions. Plus she's sweet as anything, and she makes the world's best cookies."

Rose thought about it, but only for a second. The memory of the previous night was haunting her. Maybe it was good, keeping her mind off of her grandfather's death. Whatever it was, she couldn't stop seeing it in her mind, the dogs savaging that silver stag.

"Do you think she'd talk to me?"

"Aunt Arlene? Nobody likes visitors as much as she does. Go on by, Rose. It'll be a nice distraction for both of you. She'll lighten your heart, at least for a little while."

"Maybe I will."

But she wouldn't. She'd entertained the notion, but now discarded it. Rose wasn't sure she wanted her heart lightened, and though she was sure Jenny's aunt was perfectly nice, the idea of just barging in on some stranger just to talk about wild dogs and old legends seemed more than a little crazy to her. No, she had to clean up the cabin if her parents were coming home, and she had to work tomorrow, and then there'd be the wake and the funeral.

What she'd seen was terrible. It had scared the hell out of her.

But it was over, now.

A breeze blew across the lake, rippling the surface and making the tall pines on the far shore sway. Arlene Murphy took a breath of mountain air and held it, savoring the scent and the moment. She'd already painted the water, but something had been lacking, and now she dabbed at the white on her palette and began to add the little crests and streaks wrought by the wind. Of the pines she'd only sketched in the trunks with lines done in an uneven blend of brown, yellow, and black. Adding the effects of the wind to the pines would be a simple matter.

Perfect. Her dissatisfaction with the piece evaporated. She'd left room in the painting to add a naked, sensual naiad erupting from the water, hair whipping back, spraying water. The figure thus far was merely a silver silhouette, the suggestion of face and breast and belly.

She owed Random House a book cover for a fantasy novel involving warrior monks. It would be a dark piece, full of malign intent. Arlene would bring all of her skills to bear, put her own fears and anger into it. In her mind's eye, she could already see the finished painting—could imagine how it would look on the cover of the book.

That would pay the bills.

But the publisher was going to have to wait just a while longer. This piece had come to her the previous morning, while she was on her daily hike along the shore of the lake. The exercise was invigorating, and with her cholesterol, and the twenty pounds she could never seem to get rid of, she needed it desperately. Arlene made it a rule never to start a painting the same day that the image came to her. It needed to ferment a little before she could put it on the canvas.

This one had frustrated her, until the wind had altered the scene. Now it would be all she'd hoped—bright, exultant, wild, sexy, and full of hope. Arlene had to do something to prepare for the descent into the sinister that the warrior monk painting would require. Just thinking about the image she wanted—a little bit of

Frazetta's *Death Dealer*, but mixed with James Earle Fraser's *End of the Trail*, the warrior monk hunched down low over the horse, as though nearly dead, but turning to face the unsuspecting reader with blood on his chin and on the blade of his axe—made her shiver.

Arlene forcibly drove the image from her mind. She took a breath and watched the lake again, waiting for the wind to refresh her spirit and the picture in her head of what her painting would be. After several moments, another gust came, and she breathed deeply once more. With all of the folklore, myth, and legend she had read in her life, it was simple for her to imagine herself as that naiad, bursting up from the water—made from water herself. At fifty-three, and having never worried overmuch about such things as hair and makeup, she knew most people would be amused to learn how easy it was to fantasize like this.

Those people didn't know what they were missing. And Arlene knew that she would never have been able to explain to them. Certainly there was darkness and cruelty and perversion in folklore and myth, but whenever possible, she focused on the purity and beauty to be found there, the joyfulness that existed in so many stories and figures of legend.

Arlene had spent her entire life holding her breath, feeling the presence of something just beyond her peripheral vision, turning at a sudden sound, hoping to catch sight of something wonderful. Magical. If she lived out her days never having fulfilled that hope, she could think of worse ways to have spent her time. Meanwhile, though, she brought her dreams to life on canvas.

She had become part of the scenery herself in Kingsbury, up on the mountain and by the lake, always with some painting in progress, clothes dappled with color. The people of Kingsbury loved her because her fame was twofold—partially due to her reputation as a fantasy artist, and partially due to the hundreds of paintings she'd done of Kingsbury itself—the town, the natural beauty around it. But they also treated her like everyone's favorite crazy aunt.

If not for her success as an artist, her love of folklore and utter refusal to alter her behavior no matter who was in the room—she'd met the President once, Bush number one, and neither one of them had come away too impressed—Kingsbury would have made Arlene nothing more than some odd, witchy-woman character out of a novel herself.

In a way, she thought she might have quite liked that.

Not enough to regret her success, however. To make a living by painting—and not have to worry about anything else—was a gift from whatever gods there might be.

Arlene thought there might be many. She hoped there were. The idea made the world a much more interesting place.

Again, she looked up from her canvas, took in the panorama, and set back to work. But even as she brought brush to canvas, a shiver went through her, a little frisson of pleasure and fear combined. Her breath caught in her throat. She stared at the intimate silver lines that made up the beginnings of the naiad in her painting, and shuddered.

Something was near.

Could it be today? A little, self-deprecating laugh bubbled up from her throat. She really ought to stop hoping so hard. The disappointment always left her so blue. Really, she should ignore the feeling that prickled at the back of her neck. She should not even look up until that sensation went away.

"Who'm I kidding?" she whispered to herself.

Arlene looked past the canvas, out of the woods and across the lake. She searched the surface, wondering if her painting had summoned something forth. What a dream that would be, becoming a part of folklore herself. But she saw nothing unusual on the lake.

Still, the prickle on her skin remained, that certainty that just out of sight something hovered, waiting to be seen.

Motion on the far shore drew her eye.

The sun was bright on the water, making the darkness of the shadows amongst the thick pines a deep, impenetrable charcoal. Within those shadows, just beyond the tree line, something stood and stared at her. It would have been impossible to see its eyes from this distance—this animal, or man, or thing, whatever it was—but she *felt* its attention. It had noticed her, perhaps sensing her awareness of its presence.

In the shadows, that figure was solid black—as tar, as oil, as raven's wings, all of that and darker—noticeable as a streak of pure white paint against beige.

All her life, Arlene had been holding her breath waiting for this moment—waiting to exhale—but instead, she inhaled sharply. The black figure darted left along the lakeshore, staying beyond the tree line. It moved so swiftly she caught only glimpses of its perfect darkness as it ran. So fast. Impossibly fast.

She watched for several long seconds until she could not see it any longer. Her heart beat wildly in her chest. The wind came again, but the mountain air had an earthy, slightly rotten odor now.

It's coming this way, she thought. *It's seen me, and now it's coming.*

Though she'd spent her life training herself to have faith in extraordinary things, now Arlene tried to believe that it had been nothing but a dog, or a wolf, or even a bear. It had been big enough to be a bear, she thought.

So fast.

Nothing was that fast. The lake was vast. How long would it take for the wolf to make it all the way around to this side? What a stupid thought. No wolf could have caught her scent or even seen her from that distance, all the way across the lake. She'd imagined the swift shadow. The darkness of the warrior monk assignment must have been affecting her more than she'd realized. Her senses were always open to the wondrous, and today, she'd let the sight of a shadow get the better of her.

All of her denials sounded so reasonable in her mind.

The hell of it, though, was that she still felt it. The thing had been there. And it was coming, tearing around the rim of the lake, full of malevolent intent.

Arlene had spent all those years readying herself to accept a moment such as this. Now that it had arrived, she could not pretend she did not see, did not feel, did not know...

She left the easel and the paint, but took the wet canvas, carrying it ahead of her like some enchanted shield as she hurried for her Jeep. Once she'd loaded it into the back and climbed into the driver's seat, she hesitated a moment, looking doubtfully at the easel sitting there in the midst of the trees.

But she wouldn't be back for it. Not alone, at least.

Arlene dropped the Jeep into gear and sped off across the rutted dirt road, tires kicking up a cloud of dust. Heart thundering in her chest, she tried to catch her breath, and resisted the magnetic pull of the rearview mirror. As she reached a turn in the road and spun the wheel, she reached up one hand and turned the mirror away. For the first time in her life, she was afraid of what she might see.

8

Mike finally had a design he liked for Mabel Rutherford's dining room. The problem was that the woman had been a nightmare to deal with when it came to his sketches. Some people were like that. If they saw the finished work, the actual piece of furniture, they would remark on its beauty. But for some reason it seemed to them that the existence of it as a sketch made it unfinished and felt they were almost required to find fault. That could be a long process. He'd dealt with Mrs. Rutherford before, and knew she would be difficult.

So he'd decided not to show her the sketches for her dining room. Instead, he was going to bite the bullet and make one of the chairs. If she didn't buy it, someone would. The legs and spindles would all be done with nothing but hand tools. The seat would be finished and edged and smoothed the same way, but to get the basic shape, he needed the table saw.

All day he'd worked on the sketches, and by the time he'd had something that satisfied him, it was nearly dark. He'd stopped for an hour to have something to eat and to drink several glasses of ice water. He always got dehydrated while working in the shop, even if all he was doing was sketching. It was as though the dry wood drew the moisture out of him.

Now he turned on all of the lights in the shop, and the place lit up brighter than day. Shadows were misleading when it came to riving wood, whittling spindles, and working with the adze and spokeshave and other tools. A shadow might lead him to put too much pressure on the hand plane, and then there was an indent where he hadn't meant one to be.

Mike felt a bit of moisture just beneath his nose and he reached up to touch it, alarmed at first, thinking his nose might be bleeding again. How odd that had been, last night, the way the blood had just started up without any reason. He hadn't bumped his nose or done anything to bring it on. And it had taken ten minutes of dabbing damp napkins to his nose before it had completely stopped.

This morning, when he'd set down to work on the sketches, a clearer picture in his mind of what he wanted, it had started up again, bright crimson drops spotting the sketches of Mrs. Rutherford's dining room.

But this time, there was no blood. He sniffled. *Must just be allergies,* he thought, as a way to jinx the possibility he might be getting a cold.

Studying the shelves against the back wall of the workshop, Mike picked out a piece of oak that was perfect for his needs. He folded the sketches and slid them into the back pocket of his jeans, then picked up the slab of oak and brought it over to the table saw. He checked the machine over, locked the wood down onto the table to keep it from shifting when he didn't want it to, and started up the saw.

The whine ground against his skull like the scream of a dentist's drill. Mike flinched and stood up, backing away from the table. He paused for a moment, wondering if something was wrong with the saw, but then he realized that it always sounded like this. Most days, it simply didn't bother him. He felt the whine in his head, like he was grinding his teeth. His allergies, again. Must have been. His sinuses were packed and the noise added pressure. Something like that.

But he'd only need the saw for a few minutes.

He set to work. When the saw began to cut through the wood, the whine was worse. He forced the tension of his muscles, guiding the saw, careful with the curves. The basic shape of the seat was all he needed. The rest he would do by hand.

With a pop, the power blew, casting the workshop in darkness. The whine of the saw lingered for a second, diminishing, and then there was silence as well.

"What the hell?" he asked the dark, but the only reply was the echo of his own voice.

The night was overcast, blotting out the moon and stars. There would be very little light from the windows, but after the brilliant brightness of the workshop, his eyes would need time to adjust.

The pop had sounded almost like a transformer blowing. There was one on a telephone pole just down from his place. He could see it if he looked out the window nearest the front, so he made his way over to the window, careful with each step. He was usually pretty meticulous about cleaning up after himself—safety first and all that—but just in case he'd left any wood stacked on the floor, he slid his feet forward, searching the darkness with the toes of his boots.

At the window, he looked out. The silhouette of the telephone pole was visible, darker than the night. Even with the heavy cloud cover, there was a trace of ambient light—enough to make shades of black and gray instead of pure darkness. The fat transformer box on the pole was dark and dormant. If it had blown, there were no sparks, and it had not started a fire. That was a good sign at least.

Mike took a breath and rested his forehead against the window. His momentum was gone. Without power, he couldn't get started on Mrs. Rutherford's chair. He only hoped his passion for the design hadn't changed in the morning.

As he started to turn back toward the dark workshop, he caught sight of motion outside. Out on the street, two black dogs were trotting by. They were the most enormous hounds he'd ever seen, big, sleek things with pointed ears and eyes that glistened in the dark. They passed the telephone pole, and the transformer box sent out a shower of sparks.

The dogs swung their heads from side to side as though searching for something, stopped to raise their snouts and sniff the air. One of them lowered his head and started snuffling the pavement as though following a scent. The other studied every building, every window, and the dark spaces between them.

Hunting dogs, he thought. But what were they hunting? The dog who'd been sniffing at the pavement lifted its head and swung around. Mike backpedaled from the window, suddenly afraid to have the dog see him. It seemed foolish—he was inside his house, after all—but instinct forced him away from the glass.

Ten or fifteen seconds ticked by and he took a tentative step forward. When he looked out at the night again, the dogs were gone.

A trickle came from his left nostril. Cursing his allergies, Mike reached up to wipe it away, and it smeared on his hand. He caught the coppery smell, then, and knew it wasn't his allergies this time. His nose had started to bleed again.

"Damn it," he snapped, there in the dark.

There was nothing more to be done in here tonight. All he could do was get the chair seat off of the table, and shut it down. His eyes had adjusted enough that he could make out shapes and objects in the workshop, but still he was careful making his way back to the table saw. He wiped the hem of his ratty t-shirt across his nose, but the bleeding seemed to have been just that one trickle. As he released the clamps holding the wooden seat to the table, he moved his hands slowly, gingerly, wary of the darkness. He did it all mostly by touch.

Mike slid his hands under the slab of oak.

With another pop, the power came on. He shut his eyes against the sudden brightness of lights in the workshop and the whine of the saw filled the room. The blade bit into flesh and bone. He cried out in pain jumped back from the table.

With the room lit up, the blood on the saw and the wood and the table looked too bright, too red, almost artificial. The little finger of his right hand lay on the table, strangely pale. He lifted his hand and stared at the half inch stump and the blood pulsing out of it. A strange numbness filled him. *Shock,* he thought.

And then, *Stupid.*

Mike used his left hand to switch off the saw, furious at himself for not having done so before. Safety first, what a joke. But it wasn't just stupidity. For the power to have come back on at precisely that moment, that was just dreadful luck.

He took off his t-shirt and wrapped it tightly around his hand, even as he walked over to the phone to call 911. Maybe he could drive himself to the hospital, but he didn't know how much the finger would bleed, didn't know if he'd stay conscious. And if they came quickly, maybe the paramedics could save the finger. Could be the doctors would be able to reattach it. They did stuff like that on tv all the time.

Alan teased him all the time about how one day he'd lose a finger in here. The jokes weren't going to be funny anymore.

Rose sat with one hand on the mouse, bathed in the glow of her computer screen. She'd gone back and cleaned up the cabin as best she could, putting the place in order for her parents' return, but this afternoon she'd returned to her apartment. Before dark. After last night, she didn't feel like sleeping at the cabin for a while.

The light was on in the hall, and another in the living room. Voices drifted to her from the television. She'd been in the middle of watching *Good Will Hunting* for about the twentieth time. It was old enough now to be considered an old movie—old enough to be available for free On Demand—but she loved the movie. One of her favorite moments in any film ever was when Casey Affleck, Ben's little brother, got up in the face of the arrogant Harvard jerk in the bar and said *"my boy's wicked smaht!"*

She loved that. And she loved the melancholy, working-class wisdom that Affleck was able to bring to his supporting role. He'd made enough bad decisions after so that people forgot he could really act, but *Good Will Hunting* proved it. Rose had a soft spot for Affleck. She wondered if it was because he looked a little bit like Mike Richards. On the other hand, she wondered if she had a soft spot for Mike because he looked a little bit like Ben Affleck.

She figured the truth was that she had a soft spot for Mike because he was Mike. Rose knew he had feelings for her, and she knew she felt something in return. But it didn't feel like love to her. She'd known Mike most of her life and though she knew he was a good, decent, hard-working man, in the back of her mind there would always be the goofy kid who'd snapped her bra strap like an elastic in the sixth grade and didn't think girls should play hockey.

Mike now was so completely different from Mike then. He was a man, now. A catch, her mother had told her, many times. Maybe she ought to work harder at not seeing the goofy kid in his face every time he smiled at her.

Or maybe she should just not watch *Good Will Hunting* so often.

The movie was still on in the living room. All day she'd been turning over in her mind the stricken look on her grandmother's face that morning when she'd dropped the tea cup, and the thing she'd said. Talking to Jenny had only guaranteed that Rose would continue to work the thing over in her mind. In the middle of watching the movie, she'd found herself drifting back to those thoughts again and again, until finally she just had to satisfy her curiosity.

A quick net search, that was all. She didn't even bother to pause the movie. It wasn't like she hadn't seen it before. Anyway, it would only take her a few minutes. In her bedroom, where her computer desk took up nearly all the space that wasn't occupied by bed or dresser, she hadn't taken the trouble even to turn on the light.

Now she sat in front of the screen and typed "Seven Whistlers" into Google search. There were a few references to books of folklore and legends, but not many. This didn't surprise her. Some bits of folklore made it into popular culture, but most never did.

She hit a couple of dead links before coming up with a web site that had a description of the legend. As she read, a chill spread through her.

"The Seven Whistlers are evil spirits most often mentioned in the folklore of various regions of England, primarily Worcestershire. They appear as enormous black dogs, often accompanied by loud shrieking or whistling noise, as of the wind. Legend says they are demons loosed from Hell, searching for souls upon which the devil has laid claim. They harbinger disaster and ill luck for any who encounter them. If all seven should ever gather at once, it is believed that the world will end."

Rose read the last line again, and shivered. The chill she felt would not go away.

—9—

Rose slept poorly.

Her dreams were filled with visions of huge mongrel dogs, their saliva-flecked jaws snapping hungrily as they chased her through the dark woods that surrounded Kingsbury.

The squeal of a truck's bad brakes outside her window made her eyes flutter open, and she glared at the wan morning light filtering through her bedroom window. Her legs ached as if she had run a marathon. The dread and terror of her nightmares lingered and she intended to get up right away, not wanting to descend back into dreams. Instead, she rolled over and promptly fell back to sleep.

When she woke again, her head ached and she had cottonmouth in the worst way. Reaching for the glass of water she always kept on her bedside table, she groaned as she caught sight of the clock. It was after nine o'clock. She hated sleeping late. Rose dragged herself from bed, went into the kitchen to pour herself some orange juice, and then opened her door to pick up the newspaper from her doormat. Thursday. And her grandfather was still dead, his wake and funeral yet to come. Fresh grief blossomed in her. For the first few minutes after waking, in the space between bad dreams and real life, she'd managed not to think about his death at all. But that couldn't last.

A deep sigh shuddered through her and she turned and carried the newspaper back to the kitchen. When she threw it on the table, face-down, she got a look at the headlines under the fold. One of them caught her eye.

THE WILD COMES TO TOWN

She reached for the paper again and picked it up, a chill passing through her. Rose read the story and the dread of her nightmares returned, settling into her bones. The story concerned a recent rash of reports coming into the newspaper and the police department from locals and tourists alike who'd reported seeing large, black-furred animals in the woods, around the lake, and even in town. Some had claimed to see wild dogs.

The police chief chalked it up to a long, hot summer making some food scarce, forcing bears, wolves, and even moose to forage closer to town than they would normally venture. "We've had animals in town before, and we'll have them again. That's part of the beauty of living in Kingsbury," the chief had said. "We just have to do our best to live in harmony with the wild, without anyone getting hurt."

Rose snickered. "Yeah. 'Cause it's that simple."

Then the humor drained from her. Large, black-furred animals. It was such a general description and its implications troubled her deeply. Locals would sure as hell know how to spot a wolf or a moose or a bear, but it had been the police chief to make that leap. The only animals mentioned specifically by people who'd reported sightings to the paper were wild dogs.

The memory of her Internet surfing from the night before came back full force. The legend of the Seven Whistlers had given her the creeps, but she'd told herself it was only a legend, no matter what she'd seen. Wild dogs were wild dogs. Nothing supernatural about any of it. The very idea seemed ridiculous.

But it didn't *feel* ridiculous.

She didn't have to work today, and it occurred to Rose that there might be a better way to spend the time than wallowing in her grief over her grandfather's death. Jenny had said there might be a local version of the legend, and that if there was, her Aunt Arlene would know it. Rose had brushed off the idea of going to talk to the woman yesterday.

The newspaper trembled in her hand and she dropped it, staring a moment at the way the newsprint had blackened her fingertips. She told herself that she wasn't just trying to sublimate her grief, burying it by finding something to occupy her mind. She needed to talk to Arlene Murphy, if only to remind herself that the Seven Whistlers were only a story, nothing more.

But, now that Rose had slept so late, she'd probably missed Arlene at her studio, which meant if she wanted to see the woman, she'd have to chase her down in the woods where Jenny said she did much of her painting. The idea of traipsing out in the woods troubled her. After all of the strange things she'd witnessed in the forest lately, she was leery about leaving the town center at all.

Like that's gonna work, she thought. Spend the rest of your life hiding out in town, never going into the woods again.

She wondered why the little voice in the back of her head always had to be so sarcastic.

Rose went to the bathroom and turned the shower on, waiting for steam to start clouding the glass before she stepped inside. She arched her back, working out the kinks of the night, grateful for the hot sting of the spray as the water poured over her aching body.

Most days she could be in and out of the bathroom in less than twenty minutes. Today, she could not pull herself away from the hot water and the way it released so much tension from her muscles. It was almost ten thirty by the time she finished drying her hair and put on a touch of eyeliner, mascara, and lip gloss.

Better turn in early tonight, maybe even get Jenny to give me another one of those little pills that make you sleep the sleep of the dead.

Rose shivered as the thought eddied around her brain, calling up thoughts of her grandfather's death yet again, with a sharpness that took her breath away. Though he had been lost to her for such a long time, her heart still remembered the old days, and the vibrant companion he'd been before the Alzheimer's locked him away inside his own head.

That lovely, crotchety old man was truly gone now—both body and soul—and the realization was like a lead weight, dragging her down into the gray numbness of depression.

She didn't feel like eating a real breakfast—the small kitchenette in her apartment didn't inspire much more than microwave meals and the odd grilled cheese sandwich anyway—but Rose made herself take a few bites of a strawberry Pop Tart so her stomach would stop growling. Putting the left over Pop Tart in a plastic bag, she ran the dirty dish and her juice glass under the faucet, then grabbed a bottle of water and an apple, shoving them into her backpack with the unfinished Pop Tart. If she got really hungry later, she'd have something to munch on.

Ever since she started watching her parents' cabin, she'd let her apartment go to hell. She vowed that after she'd gone up to the cabin to feed and walk Lucy, and then tracked down Arlene, she'd come home and give the place a thorough going over. Cleaning had always been a good way to clear her mind, and maybe it would wear her out enough so that she wouldn't have to medicate herself to get one good, dreamless night of sleep.

Lucy had been ecstatic to see her. The big dog had jumped all over her, spattering her navy wool sweater with a healthy coating of slobber, right up until Rose spilled food into her bowl, and then the dog had another target for her attentions.

Now, as she drove back toward town, she missed the big mutt. Rose turned up the heat in her car as she made a left onto Braeburn Street, and started the search for a parking spot. The tourists who flocked to New England for the fall foliage had made it almost impossible for the locals to find parking anywhere downtown, but Rose lucked out, finding a tiny space between a Suburban and a Mercedes Benz roadster. She squeezed her battered red Honda between them and got out.

The cool crispness of the Vermont air filled her lungs, invigorating her. It left her with a sense of wellbeing that was almost enough to make her forget her troubles for a moment. Almost.

She slung her backpack over her shoulder and crossed the street, looking for Arlene's address. Braeburn Street had only recently experienced a mini-renaissance. Once home to a mechanic's shop and the old Geary Foundry, the tiny street now boasted two art galleries and the Geary Lofts—a series of artists' studios erected on the remains of the old foundry. The previous year, the mayor had even given the street a nickname—Artists' Alley.

Rose knew this stop would likely be a waste of time, but before she went hiking around the woods up by the lake in search of Arlene Murphy, she figured she ought to at least stop at the woman's downtown studio. The way things had been going, she didn't expect it to be that simple, but better to try and come up empty than to truck around the mountain and only then discover the artist had been down here in town all along.

A shiver went through her as she found the buzzer for Arlene's loft. Rose wished she'd had the foresight to stow her woolen cap in her backpack before she'd left the apartment that morning. The temperature had been dropping steadily since morning and it was getting to be downright *cold* for autumn.

"*Yes?*" came a tinny voice from the callbox.

Rose blinked in surprise and stared for a moment at the box. A smile touched her lips as she realized she wasn't going to have to go into the woods after all. She cleared her throat, and spoke into the speaker grate.

"Hi, Miss Murphy? Arlene. I'm Rose Kerrigan, Jenny's friend? She said you might be able to help me."

"*Help you how?*" The woman's voice sounded tentative, even anxious.

"I'd rather not say out here on the street like this, if you don't mind. May I come up?"

There was a pause, as if Arlene was thinking about it. Then the buzzer on the steel-reinforced door sounded. Rose reached out and pulled open the door.

Draped in a dusky purple caftan that hung on her like a shroud, with more than a dozen strands of amethyst beads looped around her neck, Arlene Murphy reminded Rose of the aging Stevie Nicks. But when she took in her curly scarlet hair and pale skin, she decided that the artist reminded her more of some future version of Tori Amos…well, a Tori Amos who had raided Stevie Nicks' closet. She had a sage, earth-mother thing going on, combined with a no-nonsense attitude that belied her appearance.

"Would you like some tea, Rose? I was just boiling water."

"I'd love some, thanks."

Arlene went into the kitchenette. "I don't drink caffeine, so there's only herbal. I hope that suits."

"That'd be perfect, thanks."

"How do you like it?"

"However you take it is fine."

"Two Licorice Roots it is, then," Arlene replied, pouring the boiling water into a large ceramic teapot decorated with tiny penguins. "Have a seat. The tea will just be a minute."

Rose looked around the large, open room with its twin skylights and junk-strewn vanilla pine floor, and could see almost no space that had not been piled up with books, laden with scarves, or stacked with CDs. Art books lay open on tables and on the floor. Old vinyl album covers leaned against the stereo speakers but there seemed no turntable to play them. There were three medium-sized easels set up underneath the skylights, and a long white coffee table covered in painting supplies, but there didn't seem to be a place to sit comfortably without disturbing Arlene's disorder.

She decided that Arlene must have meant for her to sit on one of the thick, pink-and-yellow cushions that lay haphazardly on the floor. Plopping down, Rose set her backpack beside her, and tried to make herself comfortable.

Arlene didn't seem at all disturbed to find her guest sitting on the floor. She set the tea tray down on a box of Quash paints that took up the floor space in front of Rose and tucked her skirt underneath her so she could join her guest on the ground.

After Arlene had fixed their tea in two thick handmade clay pots, Rose hesitated, not sure how to begin.

"You said you needed my help?" Arlene prompted her with a reassuring smile.

Rose nodded. "I wanted to ask you about this story Jenny related to me. Some pretty odd things have happened to me recently and it reminded her of this legend about the Seven Whistlers—"

Arlene's features tightened, and the woman blanched.

"Are you all right?" Rose asked.

"*Of course,*" Arlene said under her breath, obviously speaking to herself and not to Rose. She set her pot down on the tea tray, then absently picked it right back up again.

"I'm sorry—" Rose began, but Arlene waved a hand at her to stop.

"Please, just a moment. You've reminded me of something. Let me think."

Rose nodded, waiting. Finally, Arlene shook her head as if to clear her thoughts, and then smiled at Rose.

"So, Jenny told you part of the legend, but didn't know it all, and figured I could fill you in on its origins. She's a sensible girl. If anyone in Kingsbury would know, it would be me. I collect legends and stories. Always have. A lot of them go into my art, but that's not the only reason they fascinate me. Guess I'm just one of those people who's always wanted to believe in the fantastic."

"So, you do know the myth?" Rose asked.

Arlene nodded.

"It's an old tale, but still very powerful," she said. Her gaze became distant as she recalled the details of the legend. When she spoke again, her voice had an ominous quality, as though to Arlene Murphy, this was more than merely a story.

"Seven hounds were dispatched from Hell to seek the Devil's due, to collect the souls of men who where damned for dreadful cowardice in the face of death. No, cowardice is not the word. That alone won't damn us, Rose. But if a man willfully sacrificed another in order to save his own life, to delay the day when the reaper might come for him, why, of course he would be damned. His soul would be forfeit because he lived on in the other's stead."

"Who would do that? That's terrible," Rose said, clutching her mug of tea tightly between her hands. The basics of the legend, she had learned from Jenny and from her online research, but this…this was new, and it got under her skin.

"You might be surprised what people will do when their lives are in peril. When the axe is about to fall, many a man—or woman—would gladly put another in his place in order to save his own life. It's a hideous thing to steal another's time on this Earth.

Unforgivable. But, listen. There's more to the tale. The seven whistlers hunt the souls of the damned, and some are cowards in death as well as in life. The hounds spread out across the Earth, but the legend says that they may come together to hunt elusive prey. It's said that should all seven hounds ever gather in one location, it will spell the end of the world as we know it...The End of Days."

Rose nodded. There were differences, but she already knew this part of the legend. Still, an icy chill raced through her. She thought of the two hounds destroying the stag in the woods outside her parents' cabin. That had been almost two days ago. She wondered how many of the hounds were in Kingsbury now.

"I've answered your question, Rose. I hope you'll answer mine. Why do you want to know about the Whistlers?"

Rose swallowed. She wanted to tell Arlene about her strange experiences in the woods, about the hounds she had seen in the darkness ripping the stag apart, and the article in the *Kingsbury Gazette* about the strange animals, but she was afraid the older woman would think she was crazy. All this talk of legends...the artist collected them, painted them. No matter how much passion she had for the stories, that didn't mean that she truly believed in them.

Still, if anyone would believe her, it would be this woman.

"You're gonna think I'm nuts, but I've seen them. The hounds, that is," Rose said quietly. "Two of them, in the woods outside my parents' cabin. Other people have seen them, too; they just don't know it. Look at the front page of today's *Gazette,* and you'll see what I'm talking about."

Arlene stared at her, the mug of tea trembling slightly in her hand as a swath of clouds passed over the skylights, casting the room into shadow. Arlene set her mug down on the tea tray and looked up at the skylights, then back at Rose. Her face was ashen.

"Believe me when I say that I would love to think creatures like the Whistlers existed in real life, but I'm afraid that they are just a figment of our ancestors' very vivid imaginations."

"You don't understand—" Rose began, but Arlene cut her off.

"Of course I understand. I just think that things like this are better left to paintings and books. Put away what you've seen, Rose. Even if what you say is true, there's nothing you could do but get in their way. And *that* you most certainly do not want to do."

—10—

Marco Ferrara and his best friend, Evergreen Knollson, were sitting cross-legged on the floor of their makeshift fort smoking a bowl when they heard something weird in the woods below them.

When they had told Marco's dad their plans for building a fort out in the woods behind the Knollson House, Cesar Ferrara had told them to put the fort high in a tree so that no wild animals would be tempted to attack them. At the time, the boys had thought he was joking, but now, almost five years later, they both had the exact same thought at the exact same time: Marco's Dad wasn't so full of crap, after all.

"What the hell was that?" Marco said, as he almost dropped the lit match he was holding in his hand. He quickly shook the tiny fire out and dropped the match head onto the wooden floor, where it promptly rolled away into a corner.

"I don't know, man," Evergreen said, his voice cracking a little.

They waited in silence, the only sound the thrumming of the woods around them. Marco sat up on his knees, trying to get a look over the walls of the fort, but Evergreen grabbed the neck of his T-shirt and yanked him back down out of sight.

"What're you doing, idiot?!"

Marco turned and glared into Evergreen's chubby face. His friend was trying to grow a mustache to impress the senior girls, but Marco thought the pathetic wisps of facial hair only made Evergreen look like a 1970s child molester.

"I'm trying to see what's down there, turd," Marco snapped.

The sound came again, and both boys shrank back from it. It was a deep, guttural bark accompanied by a sharp, reedy, whistling sound. Neither of them could think of a single animal that made a sound like *that*.

"Maybe it's a wolf, or even a bear or something, but wounded. My dad said a hurt animal can sound like a human baby sometimes," Evergreen whispered, but Marco could tell by the panicked look on his friend's face that Evergreen didn't believe a word he was saying.

"I don't know, man. I've never heard an animal sound like that before."

Evergreen's eyes lit up and he gave Marco a knowing smile. "You know what it is, man? It's the pot. It's, like, laced with acid or something. We're totally hallucinating!"

Marco shook his head.

"We can't both be hallucinating the same thing, dumb ass!"

"How do you know?" Evergreen shot back.

"Because I just know," Marco said. He'd never tripped before, but he was sure whatever they were hearing was real, not some drug-induced auditory hallucination.

"Besides, I don't care if it *is* a hallucination. I'm not taking one step outta this fort till it goes away."

"Yeah, bro, I'm with you on that one."

Evergreen nodded sagely and they settled back into silence, listening for the telltale signs of the creature's departure. After a few more minutes of silence, Marco began to relax, the tension flowing from his shoulders and neck. The reek of burnt marijuana was still strong in the air around them, and Marco decided that smoking a little bit more of it to relax himself might not be a bad idea.

He crawled over to his school backpack and slowly unzipped it, trying to keep the noise to a bare minimum. Ignoring his Calculus text, he dug farther into the inner compartment until his fingers found the tiny, knotted plastic bag they'd bought that morning from Evergreen's older sister, Holly.

Just as he brought the little baggie out into the light, the Earth below them began to shake. Or, at least, that's how it seemed at first.

"What the hell?" Marco yelped, falling back onto his ass.

"Earthquake!" Evergreen screamed, grabbing hold of a tree branch to steady himself.

There came another violent shake and Marco was thrown back against the wall of the fort, the wood splintering with the impact of his weight. He tried to grab a hold of a branch like Evergreen, but his sweaty fingers slipped on the bark and he fell backward, crashing through the already broken wooden slats.

Landing on the leaf-strewn ground with a sickening crunch, Marco cried out as his knee exploded with pain. He looked down at his leg and nearly passed out. Through his ripped jeans, he could see a meaty protrusion of bone and cartilage poking out where his knee used to be.

"Oh my God," he moaned, closing his eyes tight against the pain.

When he opened them, Marco saw Evergreen staring down at him from the wreckage of the fort, a big, chubby kid clinging to a tree for dear life.

"Ever, get down here, you prick. You've gotta get a fuckin' ambulance."

For a second, Evergreen remained frozen. Then he began to climb warily down from the ruined tree fort. Impatient and in agony, Marco railed at him to hurry—letting out a string of curses that would have made his mother faint—and glanced around, desperate, wondering how much damage the earthquake had done and how long it would take an ambulance to come.

He blinked, startled by a sudden realization. Marco couldn't see any other damage. None of the houses within view had so much as a broken window.

What the hell? Marco thought to himself, his mind spinning. *What kind of earthquake only shakes one tree?*

Wrapping her shawl tightly around her shoulders for warmth, Hester McMartin shivered. The wind had picked up considerably since she'd brought Kaylie to the park at twelve-thirty, and she was all for putting her knitting back in her bag and going home.

But when she looked over at her granddaughter standing at the top of the jungle gym, preparing to catapult herself down a length of plastic yellow slide, she felt guilty. Kaylie loved coming to the park, and playing on the gym equipment. If she called Kaylie in now, after less than an hour of play, she'd have a tantrum on her hands—and she'd never get the girl to take a nap later in the afternoon.

Between a rock and a hard place, she decided to just keep an eye on her granddaughter and the weather. If either showed signs of irritability, she'd make a beeline back to her son's house and put on one of those *Wiggles* videos Kaylie loved so much.

Since both of Kaylie's parents worked, Hester had become the de facto babysitter for her only grandchild almost from the moment she was born. Her son and daughter-in-law were very appreciative of the help, and Hester didn't mind looking after the rambunctious four-year old at all, so it worked out perfectly. She even had time to knit—her passion—when Kaylie was playing at the park or taking her afternoon nap.

As she continued her knitting, Hester got lost in the work, listening to the happy sounds of children playing. As long as the kids sounded happy and there were no cries of pain or alarm, all was right with the world. She became so involved with her knitting that Hester didn't notice the sky turning from gray to a mottled black, or the way the clouds stretched across the horizon like a battalion of angry soldiers. Nor did she see the first hailstone as it plummeted from the sky directly at her head.

The chunk of ice hit Hester squarely on the top of her skull. She flinched and reached up to touch the tender point of impact, thinking someone had been cruel enough to throw a rock at her. The second and third hailstones found their marks on her shoulder and thigh, respectively. Both hurt like the dickens, forcing her up off the park bench so that she could see where they were coming from. It took her a few moments to realize the culprit wasn't some troublesome brat, but God, himself.

"Kaylie!" Hester called, running toward the jungle gym.

Her granddaughter looked up, and the little girl's eyes went wide. Hester saw that Kaylie's eyes were fixed not on her, but *above* her. She threw herself to the left and landed hard in the dirt, scraping both knees and the palms of her hand. The massive hailstone landed with a loud thud on the spot she'd just vacated, sending bits of ice and dirt in all directions.

"Kaylie! Stay inside the jungle gym!" Hester screamed, pulling herself back up, and starting toward the slide. She caught sight of the girl cowering under the overhang where the swinging bridge connected to the monkey bars.

"Stay where you are, Kaylie! Grandma's coming for you!"

The little girl nodded, her blonde pigtails bobbing on either side of her head.

Hester threw herself under the swinging bridge, wedging her adult bulk underneath the plastic slats and nickel rivets beside her granddaughter. Clutching the terrified child to her chest, Hester looked out at the chaos that surrounded them.

Hailstones the size of softballs plummeted to the Earth, knocking leaves and branches from trees, tiles off roofs, and even a bird from the sky. The one that had nearly struck her had been as big as a melon. Hester had never seen anything so destructive in her life, and it terrified her. Cooing softly to her sobbing grandchild, she closed her eyes, and began to pray for the hailstorm to stop.

When she opened her eyes, Hester saw them—four massive, black hounds. They skirted the trees by the edge of the park, their eyes as bright as new copper pennies.

–II–

Rose spent the remainder of Thursday afternoon cleaning her apartment and washing clothes. She hadn't realized how desperate she'd become for clean clothes until she opened her underwear drawer to tidy it, and found it completely empty. The pair she had on was all she had left, and since she hated going commando, laundry duty became an instant priority. She scoured the apartment looking for dirty clothes—why did dirty socks always end up gathering dust under her bed?—then threw them in a large canvas sack that she walked to the Laundromat two streets over.

Sitting in the warm, humid Laundromat, waiting for the last of her bed linens to dry, Rose found herself wishing she was far away from Kingsbury in some tropical environ. She had never felt this way about her home before. It had been sheer anguish to live in cosmopolitan Boston while she was going to B.U.—so much so that she had quit after two semesters, immediately moved back home, and gotten the job at The Red Oak Inn.

Her parents hadn't approved of her choice, but they were fairly quiet about their disapproval. Her grandmother, on the other hand, had been very vocal. But Rose wanted to be happy, and going to school had just made her *miserable.*

She had settled back into small town life like she'd never left it, Kingsbury embracing her like the long lost child she was. Rose loved the town, and the sense of community she felt every time she walked out her front door. She had the good fortune to have great friends, too. Jenny, Mike, and Alan had become her surrogate family. If she ever needed their help, or had a problem she couldn't solve on her own, Rose knew they'd be there for her no questions asked. It made her heart lighter just thinking about how safe their friendship made her feel.

If Jenny hadn't been there to hold her up, on the night she'd found out about her grandfather's death, she didn't know what she would have done. Death was life's schoolyard bully. One of these days, it would catch you alone, and then you were shit out of luck. But you still had to stand your ground, keep your chin up. Being afraid was okay; totally natural. But you couldn't run from it for very long. Standing your ground in the face of Death was a hell of a lot easier when you had friends who'd stand there with you, just as afraid, but just as unwilling to run.

Rose was still sitting in the Laundromat when her cell phone rang. She recognized the number and answered immediately, Jenny's calm voice filling her ear, and making her feel instantly better.

"The Pennywhistle. Tonight. Six o'clock. Be there or Alan and I get the 'stang out, and hunt you down."

Rose had to smile. Jenny had a way of always saying the right thing at the right time.

"No need to get the 'stang all hot and bothered," Rose giggled.

"I'll be there. Besides, there's some stuff I wanted to run by you guys tonight anyway."

"Good," Jenny said. "Oh, shoot. I gotta run. Someone's yelling in my kitchen, and I'm trying to raise mini-chocolate soufflés for the dinner menu tonight."

"Go look after your soufflés. I'll see you later."

She punched the *end* button on her cell, then pulled her bed sheets out of the dryer and began to fold them. She didn't know how she was going to broach the subject, but the strange happenings in Kingsbury needed to be addressed one way or another.

Mike was running late—later than even he had expected. His finger hurt like hell, and changing the dressing like the nurse at the emergency room had shown him had proven to be a lot trickier than he had anticipated.

The nurse had also given him a full bottle of extra strength Vicodin, which was a lot easier to manipulate than the gauze and tape, but he'd taken one of the little devils that afternoon and it had barely made a dent in the ache. Since the stuff wasn't really working for him anyway, and he wanted to drink tonight, he'd forgone taking another dose in the evening. He figured two or three Black and Tans would do a fine job of taking the edge off his pain.

The Pennywhistle was swinging when Mike pushed open the double doors and stepped inside. The air was thick with conversation and liquor…and something else Mike couldn't put his finger on. He spied Alan, Rose, and Jenny sitting in their usual spot in the back of the bar, already knee deep into their first round. Mike gave them a nod, then sauntered over to the bar where one of Dave's latest barmaids, Elektra, was manning the taps. She was a buxom girl from Greece. Elektra and her twin sister, Leni, were spending a year abroad, touring America and working odd jobs here and there for cash.

The Pennywhistle was notorious for its barmaids. The owner, Dave, had an eye for the ladies, and he was always hiring the prettiest specimens he could find. Local guys flocked to the bar, making a sport of seeing who could score with the new hires.

Dave knew that men who needed confidence needed liquor, so his hiring practices had a *very positive effect on trade. More customers, drinking more. Business was so good these days, Mike had heard that the owner of the Pennywhistle had even talked of retiring early to the Florida Keys, putting the sailboat he'd bought on a whim at a government auction in Montpelier to good use.*

Elektra gave Mike a wink as she grabbed a tall glass and started pouring his favorite. She had never said as much as two words to him, but he got the feeling if he were ever interested, she'd be willing. Maybe he was fooling himself, but the self-deception felt good, if that was the case. Elektra slipped the glass onto a coaster and slid it toward him, brushing his good hand with the side of her palm.

If this wasn't an invitation, he didn't know what was. Flattered, he left her a three-dollar tip, which she expertly slipped into very enticing cleavage.

Maybe she just knows how to play the game better than I do, Mike thought to himself, retracting his earlier inclination as he watched her ply the next guy with the same inviting smile she'd just used on him. Shaking his head in wonder at the female species—and his complete and utter lack of understanding where they were concerned—he walked over to his friends' table and sat down. At least here, he knew where he stood: Jenny was taken, and Rose...well, Rose was just Rose.

"We've got a lot more to worry about than just wolves and bears picking our trash," Rose was saying when Mike tuned in to the conversation.

It took him a few seconds to figure out what she was talking about, and then he remembered the front page of the *Gazette* from that morning.

"She's right," Mike said, taking a sip of his Black and Tan. The head tickled his nose, making him almost sneeze his next words.

"I've seen them, and believe me, they're not wolves."

"You saw them, too," Rose said, almost breathless with some combination of surprise and relief.

"Yeah, When I did this," he said, holding up his bandaged hand. Everyone gasped.

"What the hell happened to you, Mike Richards?" Jenny demanded as she leaned forward in her seat to get a better look at his gauze-wrapped right hand. After the doctor had sewn the missing piece back on, he'd wrapped the whole of Mike's hand to keep the finger stable, and Mike had repeated the process after he'd changed the dressing,

"Little fight broke out between the table saw and my pinky finger," Mike replied. "Finger got the worst of it, and I don't think anyone's hoping for a rematch. As for these animals, I saw two of them—biggest damn dogs I ever laid eyes on—right before it happened. Wolves, my ass."

"Is your hand gonna be okay?" Rose asked.

Mike grinned. It pleased him that Rose would worry about him. If he'd known cutting off a body part would get the girl's attention, he would have done it ages ago. Or not. But it still felt nice, the way Rose was looking at him. Almost enough to dull the pain.

"The doc at the emergency room said I'd gotten to him just in time," Mike said. "The EMTs were smart enough to put my pinky on ice, so they were able to reattach the tip—"

Alan shook his head in wonder.

"Didn't I warn you about takin' a finger off, man?"

Jenny smacked Alan hard on the arm, motherly concern and annoyance etched on her face.

"Alan Scott Bryce, put a little brain back in your head! Mike nearly lost his hand, and you're making jokes!"

Alan grinned sheepishly. "Not my fault he can't keep his fingers attached—"

Jenny whacked him again, and then they were off and running. All they needed was a catalyst to incite the playful couple bickering that usually made Mike feel like he was an outsider. He turned to Rose, hoping to catch her eye, see if the affection between their friends distanced her in the same way, but her dark eyes were lost in thought.

Mike noted the worried set of her brow, the way she was slowly shredding a paper drink napkin between her fingers, and reached out, touching her softly on the shoulder. She jumped, instinctively tensing at his touch.

"You okay?"

Rose blinked, and then her eyes cleared and she shook her head, an embarrassed frown turning down the corners of her mouth.

"Fine. Just thinking, that's all."

Mike sensed there was more to this than Rose was saying, but he didn't want to push the issue and make her feel like he was trying to push her away or intrude on her private thoughts, so he just shrugged, playing the moment off like it was any other.

"No worries. You need another drink?" he said, gesturing to her empty glass.

She shook her head. "I think I'm good, but thanks for asking."

She turned away, back to her thoughts, a sad, distracted look on her beautiful face. Mike found himself wishing for the days when Rose was just a face in the crowd…because it was killing him to be her friend.

Rose declined Jenny's offer to spend the night.

Her thoughts were too chaotic to deal with entertaining another person. She had to go up to the cabin to feed Lucy and let her out. By the time Lucy had done her business and scampered back into the cabin, Rose felt exhausted. All she wanted was to crawl under her parents' down comforter and think. She had a moment of trepidation as she thought of the hounds, but it seemed like they were just as likely to show up downtown as in the woods, and there was no reason for her to think they'd come back to this very spot. Rose knew she was as safe here as she would be anywhere else in Kingsbury.

Her own safety was not what troubled her.

Ideas had been whirling in her mind for hours. At first, she'd pushed them away, thinking they were crazy. But now, as she tried to relax and let sleep take her, she began to realize that they were not crazy ideas at all—they were purely logical connections she had only just begun to make.

And they terrified her.

If she was right, it would change everything.

—12—

The alarm clock went off at seven, but Rose was already awake. She'd been lying awake since half past four, scrunched up between the thick down comforter and Lucy, turning her thoughts over and over in her head. Once again she had been having horrible nightmares—crazy dreams that even now, hours after she'd woken, still upset her. She hadn't wanted to go back to sleep after that, so she'd laid there in the darkened cabin, listening to the night sounds and the conflict that raged in her own heart.

Now, though, Rose got out of bed and quickly dressed, not bothering to shower. She had questions that required answers, and she was determined to find them before her grandfather's wake later that evening.

While she fed Lucy, she sipped at a cup of tea, but her stomach was in such knots that she didn't dare try and eat anything. She didn't have time to spend the morning in the bathroom retching it back up.

As she stood by the kitchen sink watching Lucy wolf down her breakfast, she stared at the teacup in her hand. She couldn't believe it was only two days ago that she sat in this very kitchen watching her grandmother freak out at the mention of the Seven Whistlers.

What a fool she'd been not to have put the pieces together sooner. Although, if she really was honest with herself, it seemed more likely that she didn't *want* *to* see the truth than that she couldn't. It had hit her hard last night, like lightning. Something Mike had said had jarred her memory, and the image of her grandmother gripping that tea cup right before she dropped it, her skeletal fingers clutching at the cup as if it was somehow keeping her tethered to reality, had risen up in her mind, and wouldn't leave.

Her grandfather had died. The Whistlers had come to Kingsbury. Now that Rose had begun to believe that these beasts were not simply the wild dogs the chief of police wanted the town to think they were, now that she knew the legend…well, once she'd remembered her grandmother's reaction that day, how could she not have begun to think the worst.

God, it was the worst.

Rose felt certain that her grandmother knew *exactly* why the seven Hounds from Hell were in Kingsbury…and whose soul they sought.

The gravel drive crunched under her shoes as Rose climbed the last few feet to the front door of the Glen Valley Rest Home. She slipped her hand around the door pull, and slid open the opaque glass door, noting—for what she hoped was the last time—the way the name of the place was haphazardly stenciled in thick black courier across the top half of the smoky glass.

The heat was on inside, turned up high to contend with the thin blood of the ancient human relics living out their final years or months or days there. Closing the door behind her, Rose slipped off her thick jean jacket, and wrapped it around her waist. She walked over to the reception desk, her shoes squeaking on the institutional gray linoleum floor. The nurse behind the desk looked up and smiled, recognizing Rose instantly. Then the woman seemed to remember that Rose wasn't here for a visit, that there was no one here for the girl to see anymore.

She put down the file she was holding and gave Rose a sympathetic half-smile.

"Oh my goodness, Rose, I'm so sorry about your grandfather."

Rose smiled back at the woman, letting her know it was okay. "Thanks, Viola. I appreciate that. It's been rough, but we're doing all right."

Viola nodded, her thin, angular face bobbing up and down on her pencil-thin frame. Rose had often envied the nurse her boyish figure; still did, even now.

"I was wondering if my grandmother had picked up Grandad's stuff yet. She asked me to come by days ago, but I just couldn't yet, you know?"

Viola nodded vigorously. "I completely understand. A shock like that can really knock you for a loop. Let me look, but I'm almost positive we boxed up his stuff and put it in the basement."

The nurse looked down, eyes scanning the desk until they spied the black, leather-bound patient logbook. Flipping through the stiff pages, she found what she was looking for, and gave Rose a nod.

"It's here," she said. "I'll just have Bill go down and get it for you."

Rose waited in the reception area, her spine straight against the back of a sturdy wooden chair. Her head throbbed and her heart raced, making her feel queasy. From the moment she'd stepped through the door of the rest home, a terrible dread had nestled down inside her. It made her skin crawl.

The place was rank with the stink of death and infirmity. It filled her throat and nose, so that she almost couldn't breathe. She didn't know why the place had never affected her this way before. Maybe because she'd been filled with hope when she was visiting her grandfather; hope that he would get better, that he would again be the man she had known.

"Got them for you," a voice called from behind her. Rose turned in her chair to see Bill, the facility's aging caretaker, coming down the hall with two boxes under his arm.

Rose almost cried when she saw how little was left to show for her grandfather's life. Forcing back the tears that threatened to leak down her cheeks, she mustered a *thank you* for Bill.

He set the boxes down in the chair beside her and took off his cap, letting it dangle at his side. His wizened brown skin glowed like caramel under the fluorescent lights, and Rose found her heart breaking just a little more under his sympathetic gaze.

"I was real sorry to hear about your grandad, Rose," he said. "He was a nice man, and I know you all will miss him greatly."

Rose didn't trust herself to speak. She wanted to let the old man know how much his sympathy meant to her, but she also didn't want to cry.

He held out his hand. "You don't gotta say anything. I just wish there was more for you to take with you," Bill said, indicating the two small boxes.

"Thank you," she managed. "Me, too."

Bill watched as she retrieved the boxes, slipping them under her arm. She gave him a wave as she turned, and walked toward the front door.

The old man stood in the hall long after the girl had gone, watching the spot where she'd disappeared through the door. Trouble followed that girl. He could taste the darkness that dogged her every step.

He only wished he knew how to help her.

The sound of the knife slicing through the heavy packing tape was very satisfying. Rose slipped the blade under the side flap of the box, and eased it through the rest of the tape, letting the box open of its own accord.

She took out the contents, carefully arranging them on her kitchen table. When she was done, she let her knife dance across the second box. She repeated the process, until her tabletop was covered with the meager remains of her grandfather's life.

Not nearly enough to show for a man's life.

Rose went through his clothes first. There was really only some underwear, a few t-shirts, pajamas, and two pair of faded khakis. She folded the clothes and put them back in the box. The whole thing was so depressing she wanted to cry.

She picked up his watch and wallet next. The wallet was empty, except for a picture of her grandmother. It was an old picture—her grandmother was probably only in her early twenties—but it could be no one else. The young woman in the picture had the same sharp, beautiful features and hard-set mouth. Rose touched her own mouth, feeling smooth softness, where her Grandmother's young face was tense and drawn.

Rose put the wallet and watch back into the box, her hands drawn instinctively to the small cache of papers she'd set aside earlier. There was a small moleskin notebook mixed in with the hospital records, and other paper detritus. She picked up the notebook, and flipped it open. Her grandfather's spidery handwriting covered the yellowed pages.

The date on the top of the first page was January 20th 1943. Rose bit her nail, somehow certain that this was what she had been looking for.

She began to read.

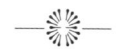

January 20th 1943

I've been shipboard for less than two weeks, but I can already feel my body beginning to settle into the rhythm of the sea. It's infernally hot below deck. Some of the guys on laundry detail sweat so much they work in their underwear. I'm just glad Momma's not here to see this, she'd whoop them all for being disrespectful.

The ship's so big, and gets dirty so fast, that it takes all two thousand of us working non-stop to keep it clean. Scrubbing isn't woman's work here, nor is cooking, nor doing wash.

Davey has the bunk below mine. It's nice to have a friend from home on board with me. We've made a few other friends, but Davey and I stick together anyway. One of the other guys asked if we were brothers. Davey just laughed, but here in the middle of nowhere I feel like we're almost that close.

Got a letter from Doris. The kid thinks she's in love with me. I told her before I shipped out that we were just friends, but at least she writes. That's nice. Davey got two letters from Isobel. I could smell her perfume when he opened them.

Wish she was writing to me.

Rose made herself a cup of tea, sipping it as she made her way through the journal entries, utterly enthralled by even the most mundane details about her grandfather's experience during World War II on the battleship *North Carolina*. He'd spent his days working and training, his nights on duty, watching for enemy aircraft as the ship trolled the waters of the South Pacific.

Her heart had skipped when she'd first encountered her grandmother Isobel's name scratched into the little moleskin journal. She'd had no idea her grandfather had married his best friend's girl. She wondered how that had come to pass.

105

March 25th 1945

We started shelling Okinawa yesterday. I keep thinking about all the civilians there, wondering if they're going to be all right. Davey says they deserve what's coming to 'em, but I don't know. The Japs are the bad guys, that's for certain, but I just don't know.

My mind keeps going back to better times, when we weren't preparing for this battle. When you could just sit out on your watch looking at the stars in the sky. What you see out on the water is like nothing you could ever see on land.

Makes you almost believe in magic when you're alone out here on the sea.

April 6th 1945

Dear God, what have I done? Davey is dead and it's my fault.

April 6th 1945—Later

We were firing at a bunch of crazy Jap pilots. Kamikazes, they call 'em. The bastards crash into you, dying as they take you down with 'em. It was near the craziest thing I ever heard about until I saw it for the first time. Chilled my heart.

The air was full of the stink of battle, guns going off all around us, on our ship, and the carriers near us in the water. I just remember hearing a loud crack in the air, and then there was smoke everywhere.

We were hit by friendly fire I heard later, but at first, I thought one of them kamikaze planes had hit us. There was blood all over everywhere, on the deck, just everywhere.

I didn't see the guy until he was almost on top of me. One of my shipmates, covered in blood. He threw himself at me, his eyes bugging out of his head. He'd been hit by shrapnel or something, so that his face was ruined and I couldn't even have said if I recognized him or not. Maybe it was the pain or the blood or the smoke, or maybe his fear just snapped something in his head, but he'd lost it.

The sailor attacked me, drove me down on the deck. He hit me a few times, then grabbed my head in his hands and started slamming me against the deck. His blood was everywhere. I didn't know what to do. I started screaming for help, but none came. I found my hands around the man's throat, and then I was choking him, trying to force him off me. He thrashed in my hands, and then suddenly, he was still.

I pushed him off me, and rolled him over, checking for a pulse. There was nothing. I didn't know what to do. The first thing that came into my head was to just roll him off the side. The ocean would take him, I thought. Just one more sailor, lost in the war...not killed by my own hands.

I got the man to the side, but as I started to push him over, I heard Davey's voice through the smoke, shouting my name. He'd come looking to make sure I was okay. I didn't know what to do. I couldn't let him find me kneeling over the corpse of one of our shipmates. Self-defense or not—and it was, sweet Jesus, it was—I'd taken a life.

I backed off quickly, slipping away in the smoke, hiding behind one of the big guns. Davey was just a figure in the smoke. He nearly tripped over the dead sailor. But then, as he knelt beside the still form, laying in that bloody mess on the deck, the smoke cleared.

A pair of sailors came up just behind him, and then one of the deck officers. I heard a voice ask Davey what had happened, and moments later, another voice saying the sailor had marks on his throat, that it looked like he'd been strangled.

God, help me, but they thought Davey had killed him.

I knew I had to step forward right then and set them straight, explain how it had all happened. But it would mean a court martial, and if they didn't believe it had been unavoidable, that it had been self defense—if they found that I'd committed murder—the penalty in court martial would be death.

I wanted to speak up, to tell the truth. I just couldn't get my voice to work.

This was the last entry. Rose reread it twice before she had to put it down. Her hands were shaking that much.

—13—

Arlene's studio was a mess. She'd spent the whole of the morning working on the book cover, the one with the warrior monk. Only now, the monk had four Hell Hounds surrounding him, waiting to go do his bidding.

She had no idea why she'd added them to the painting. There were no Hell Hounds in the book she was creating the painting for. She'd have to do a lot of fast-talking with the publisher to get them to okay it. Or not. At the moment, she found that she didn't really care *what* the publisher said. She liked the painting as it was, felt the energy the subject matter invoked as she ran her brush across the canvas.

A chill went through her, even though the heat was going full blast. She was getting antsy. Too much time with the paintings, and she always went a little stir crazy. Still, this painting unsettled her, made her feel strange whenever she looked at it. Only a fool would have failed to see why she had included the hounds. Their presence lingered in her mind, both the memory of having seen them at the lake, and the knowledge that others had seen them as well.

Her stomach rumbled, angry that she'd only fed it egg whites and a bagel this morning instead of her usual corned beef hash and scrambled eggs. The culinary arts ran strong in her family. Arlene had been thrilled when her niece, Jenny, had gotten the job as chef over at the Red Oak Inn. Some of her friends had told her that the inn had been upgraded in most travel guides from three to four stars, just based on Jenny's cooking and the influence she'd had on the menu and the kitchen.

After putting a few more strokes of paint onto the canvas, Arlene decided to let the painting to dry a bit, and go over to the Thistle Café for an early lunch. She cleaned her brushes—the one thing in her life she was meticulous with was her brushes. She loved to see them all lined up in a row waiting for her in the morning.

Her boots were waiting for her under the coffee table. There was a dab of bright blue on the toe of one of the little Ugg slip-ons. She liked it that way, she decided, not bothering to clean the leather. Arlene flipped the switch on the overhead track lighting before she slipped out, locking the door behind her.

The painting seemed to shimmer in the semi-darkness.

The Thistle Café had very few customers at eleven thirty. Arlene went over to one of the corner booths, and slid onto one of the Naugahyde seats, liking the smoothness of the material. Naugahyde had so much of leather's character, but was somehow glossier. As old-fashioned faux as it was—lending the café an inescapable old diner ambiance—Arlene had always loved it. Heck, she liked bad faux-wooden paneling, too. Nostalgia, she supposed.

She went through the menu, her eyes alighting on the Cobb salad immediately. When the girl came to take her order, she got the salad and an herbal tea, then leaned back in the booth, and waited. Her mind instantly dredged up an image of Rose Kerrigan's face. A flicker of guilt went through her as she thought about how dismissive she'd been toward Rose yesterday.

Guilt had been haunting her ever since. Arlene knew she ought to have told Rose the truth, not only what she had seen, but what she believed. Not just to appease her guilt, but because she had an idea that Rose might actually have the courage to try to do something about it.

Someone had to, or the town of Kingsbury was in deep shit. And that would only be the beginning. If all seven came together...

The waitress brought her tea, and Arlene felt absurdly grateful. It was too hot, but she sipped it anyway and wrapped her hands around the cup, borrowing its warmth. The cold she felt came both from the season and from within her. She could wrap herself in thick sweaters and jackets to combat the autumn chill, but the coldness inside her could not be escaped.

Arlene had spent her life delving into the supernatural. Not because she wanted power, or wealth and fame, but because she was just plain old curious about the subject. Magic and myth and legend. It filled her with such hope, such pleasure. She remembered being a little girl, tucked away in a lonely corner of the library, reading about dragons and ogres, trolls and werewolves, vampires and ghosts. She'd been enthralled by the tales—the myths and legends that were strangely synchronistic all over the world. It made her think that there had to be some validity to them if the same creatures that haunted Romania, also terrified the inhabitants of Peru.

111

Until now, she'd always *wanted* there to be truth in those legends.

Lost in thought, she sipped her tea again.

A wailing cry filled the café, the hysterical cry of a young child, and she spilled hot tea on her fingers. Arlene hissed as she put the cup down, quickly grabbing up her napkin to wipe off her hands, which throbbed with the scalding they'd received.

She looked over and saw a young tourist couple and their two small children standing in the doorway of the café. The young mother held a screaming, red-faced toddler in her arms, trying to quiet the child with shushes and kisses. The man had the hand of the other child, a little boy no older than five or six. The kid's face was pale, and shed tears were slowly drying on his cheeks and chin.

The waitress carried Arlene's Cobb salad toward the table, but was flagged by the woman with the now sobbing, snuffling toddler in her arms.

"We'd like a table, please?" the woman said, and Arlene realized she was almost as upset as the children. The husband remained calm, but his expression was grim.

"Sit wherever you'd like, m'am," the waitress replied. "I'll be with you quick as I can."

The couple walked to the nearest table, and the woman sat down, the child still in her lap. Arlene watched them, curious as to what had upset them so much.

"Here you are," the waitress said, setting the salad on the table in front of her.

"Thanks," Arlene said, distracted by her curiosity.

She waited as the waitress took the family's drink order and disappeared back into the kitchen. Arlene watched them. The husband glanced up from his menu and caught her eyes. She offered a sympathetic smile and he nodded his thanks.

"Are you folks all right?" she asked.

The woman glanced over at her. When she saw Arlene's honest curiosity and concern, she let out a shuddering breath and nodded.

"I think so, thank God. We were out in the woods, near that famous inn, the Five Oaks or something." Her eyes were wide as she spoke, and a bit wild. The memory of her fear was fresh. "These animals came after us. We could've been killed!"

Arlene's throat went dry.

"I'm so sorry," she said, heart heavy with dread. "Have you called the police?"

The husband looked embarrassed. "It wasn't as serious as all that. My wife thought she saw something in the woods over by the stables."

The woman glared at him.

"It wasn't *serious,* Jimmy? You saw the horses! They were going berserk in their stalls!"

The toddler sensed her mother's mood and began to cry. The woman leaned forward, and tenderly shushed her.

"Big horse dogs…" the little boy whispered to himself.

Arlene looked at him. "What did you say, little one?"

The little boy shook his head, his mouth firmly shut.

"He said they were horse dogs," the mother said. "And I'm not sure he's wrong. They were absolutely huge. Five of them. Waiting to attack us as we were going across the parking lot from the stables."

"Kelly," the husband said. "Please…"

But Arlene had stopped listening.

Five already. Five of seven. Rose was right, lord help us.

Arlene had to find Rose, and tell her what she knew, before it was too late.

–14–

Autumn leaves skittered across the parking lot of the Norton Funeral Home as Rose walked toward the front steps. She wished the breeze would carry her away as well. A group of people stood at the base of the brick and granite steps, a social circle of necessity, brought together by cigarettes. Steve LeBeau, who'd once worked for her grandfather, stood with Sally Logan, who'd grown up in the house next door. Twenty years younger, Sally wouldn't have given a disheveled old man like LeBeau a second glance, never mind spoken to him, if they weren't both shivering out in the cold for the sake of a nicotine fix.

Rose nodded politely when they greeted her, a fragile smile plastered to her face. Between the cold wind and her grief, her expression felt as though it had been cast from ceramic. Other smokers lingered outside the door and as they offered her their condolences she muttered replies and returned reassuring grasps on autopilot.

Once she entered the funeral home, the smell of the place assailed her, dozens of floral arrangements competing with the scent of baby-powdered death. A sea of faces surrounded her, many familiar, but others not. Friends of her parents, neighbors and co-workers, the elderly folks who had been playing cards and trading dinner parties and gossip with her grandparents for decades, and now patiently awaited the night when the flowers would be for them, when the little plastic letters on the sign outside the door would spell out their names.

Her gaze searched the corridor for her grandmother, Isobel. Mike Richards stopped her and gave her a quick, understanding embrace. He kissed the top of her head. Rose managed to smile up at him and she reached up to gently touch his face, but she could not hear a word he said. She felt sure she must have thanked him before she wandered away, but if not, she'd apologize another day. If there was another day.

The clock read twenty after seven. The wake would last until nine p.m. Jenny had promised to sneak off from the Inn once the dinner crowd had started to thin, but Rose would be gone from here by then.

On the right, the arched entrance to the viewing room beckoned. The floral aroma emanated even more strongly from within, along with the low chatter of mourners trading stories about the late, lamented Walter Hartung, her grandfather. They'd savor the good memories he had given them, grieve for his loss, and then move on, hoping it would be a while before they had to come back to this place.

The heat ticked from the radiator in the corner of the viewing room. Rose nodded and muttered to dozens of people, knowing they would forgive her remoteness and chalk it up to grief. She found she did not care. She eased around clusters of people and then between two distant cousins who tried to engage her in conversation. Rose barely looked at them.

For the first time since entering the room, she had an unobstructed view of the casket. The figure laying there on cream-colored silk didn't look a thing like her grandfather. No way could that be Walt Hartung. Sure, he had the same slightly hooked nose and the same thinning hair. The facial structure was right and the peaceful expression on his face must have been meant to comfort those he'd left behind. But the husk that lay there in the casket looked more like a wax figure from Madame Tussaud's than a man.

Of course it's not him, she thought. *Grandad's gone.*

And just as quickly, she realized she was glad that she would never have another chance to speak with him. If death hadn't already claimed him, she'd have asked him about his journal, about what happened to Davey Chapman, and Rose knew that whether he had lied to her or told the truth, she would have hated him for it.

Now, all she could do was mourn, both because she had lost him, and because he had never been the man she'd imagined him to be.

Isobel stood beside the casket, greeting those who had come to pay their respects with a tight smile or a sad nod, accepting their attentions and affections as her due. The stalwart widow. Rose hated to be so cold, but she could not escape the thought that the role fit her grandmother well.

The old woman glanced over and saw her, and for a moment the two of them only stared at one another. Then Isobel beckoned her, an unspoken admonition on her face, silently chiding Rose for her tardiness. Her parents' plane would be landing later tonight, so that they would be there for the funeral in the morning, but Rose ought to have been there on time to stand beside her and receive their guests.

All this passed between them in an instant.

Rose strode toward her. Someone spoke to her, put a hand on her arm, but she shook it off. Her grandmother gracefully accepted a kiss on the cheek from a woman far older and more withered than Isobel herself would ever be. A middle-aged couple—friends of her parents from down in Brattleboro—were next in line. Rose stepped between them and her grandmother, giving them her back without apology. Her grandmother's eyes lit up with anger at this affront and her glare demanded an explanation.

"There are five, now," Rose said, her voice low, but firm. Anger and fear had conspired to give her strength.

Her grandmother pursed her lips in typical disapproval. "What are you talking about, dear? You ought to have been here an hour ago."

Rose reached out and grasped her hand. The old woman's skin was thin and dry as parchment. Her grandmother flinched at this breach of protocol and fury flickered in her eyes. She did not like to be handled.

"I said there are five of them, now, Grandmother. Five of the Whistlers, here in Kingsbury."

Arlene Murphy had called Rose that afternoon with the news. It had not been welcome. All along, Rose had thought that she would feel better if only she had someone to confide in, someone who believed her, someone who would tell her she wasn't being crazy. That it was all true. She'd been wrong about that. Having her worst fears confirmed didn't make her feel at all better. It made her feel sick.

"You're babbling, Rose," Isobel said.

But Rose saw the fear in her grandmother's eyes and felt the way her fingers flinched at the news. The woman had always been pale, but one thing she had never done was let her granddaughter stare her down.

When Isobel looked away, though it was only for a moment, Rose knew that there could be no mistake, and no more doubt. Not only was it all true, but her grandmother had known what could happen. Somehow, Walt and Isobel Hartung had come upon the legend of the Seven Whistlers and had learned that it was all too real. There would be a story there, Rose knew. Perhaps they had seen one of the Whistlers before, seen someone else pay the price for their cowardice and sin. But Rose found that she didn't care about the how, or the why. In the scheme of things, it was enough to know that it must have happened, and that something, now, had to be done.

Rose stepped in close to her, ignoring the whispers around her.

"I found his journal," she said, her voice low. "I know."

Her grandmother lifted her eyes and there was ice there. "What do you think you know?"

Anguish swept through Rose. She forced back the tears that threatened to spill down her face, but when she spoke, her voice quavered.

"I know what happened to Davey Chapman," she whispered. Her grandmother flinched at the utterance of that name. "I know you were supposed to be his girlfriend, but you married Granddad instead. Maybe you didn't know when you married him that he'd let Davey die in his place, but at some point, you found out."

"Lies," her grandmother hissed.

Like a cornered animal, she gazed around at the mourners who were close enough to have heard at least some of what had been said. Then she turned away, as though she could simply pretend that Rose wasn't there.

"They keep coming, and that means they haven't gotten what they're searching for," Rose whispered. She held her grandmother's wrist, now, holding the woman close to her, not letting her step away. Isobel would not look at her, but Rose didn't care.

She gnawed her lower lip and squeezed the old woman's wrist. "You're hiding it, Grandmother. You're hiding *him*. That's the only way I can figure it. Who else would try to keep them from claiming his...his soul?"

Rose rasped this last word, and now she could not have spoken above that tiny whisper if she'd wanted to. All her grief and disillusionment crashed over her and she felt her legs weaken. Even after what he'd done, those many years ago, if there had been a way to save her Granddad somehow, she'd have done it. No matter what. She loved him enough, even now, to give herself in his place, if they would have taken her. But the Whistlers hadn't come for Rose. They'd come for Walt Hartung. And if they didn't get him...

"If they don't get what they came for," Rose said, steadying her voice, releasing her grip on the bitter, pinched old woman's wrist, "all of the ugly stuff that's been happening in town is going to continue. It's going to get worse. People are going to die. And the hounds will keep coming. There are five here already. Two more, and then it's over for everyone.

"Even after what he did," she went on, staring at Isobel, "I can't believe he's the kind of man who'd let the rest of us die for it."

Her grandmother glared at her. A rare tear sparkled upon her powdered cheek. She stepped over to the open casket and lowered herself gingerly to the kneeler, to say a prayer over her dead husband's remains. The visitors had cleared away, at last sensitive enough to let the grieving wife and granddaughter of the dead man sort out their troubles alone. They had the front of the room to themselves.

"Is that really the man he was?" Rose asked, almost afraid of the answer.

Isobel turned, hatred etched upon her face. "Go, damn you! Get out!"

Rose hesitated, but only for a second. "Fine. I'll figure it out myself. I'm not going to let this happen."

She turned on her heel and fled the funeral home, people clearing a path for her, gaping in astonishment. Some well-intentioned woman reached out to her and Rose nearly crumbled at that offer of tenderness. Instead, she shook her head and forged on.

When she banged the front door open, the smokers jumped. One of them swore and dropped his lit cigarette. Rose ignored them, and headed for her car, keys out and jangling in her hand.

As she opened the door, someone gripped her arm. She twisted out of the grasp and spun around, furious, only to find herself face to face with Mike Richards.

"Rose," he said, searching her eyes, "didn't you hear me calling after you?"

She hadn't.

"Mike, I can't...I've gotta go."

His took her hand, firm and gentle all at once, gazing intensely at her, eyes full of purpose.

"What is it, Rose? What's wrong?"

For a moment she almost pushed him away. But those eyes trapped her.

"You'd never believe me."

"Yeah," he said immediately, nodding. "Yeah, I would, Rose. I'm not some bystander, here. I know you. I'll believe you."

She remembered the way he'd talked about the hounds the night before, and how spooked he'd been by his encounter with them on the night he'd sliced his finger on the table saw in his workshop. *Maybe you will,* she thought. *Maybe you will.*

"Look, we're friends, right?" Mike said. "Whatever it is, let me help."

Rose glanced back at the funeral home and flinched in surprise as she saw her grandmother standing on the stairs amongst the smokers. Isobel had followed her out. The old woman stared at her and Mike with narrowed eyes, full of suspicion.

"Get in the car," Rose said.

Mike blinked. "Okay. Where are we going?"

"Just get in. I'll explain on the way."

As she started up the car and pulled out of the parking lot, Rose glanced in the rearview mirror. Several people had followed her grandmother out and were trying to talk to her, but Isobel only waved them back as she walked toward her car, probably telling them she'd return in a moment, thanking them for her concern.

But she wouldn't be back.

Rose was headed to her grandparents' house, and Isobel knew it. The old woman meant to stop her.

−15−

Rose pulled to a stop in front of her grandmother's house, and she killed the ignition. For a moment she and Mike just sat there listening to the engine cool. The house was dark, but seemed to beckon to her in a way it hadn't in a very long time. Ever since her grandfather had been put into the nursing home, this hadn't been his house anymore. Now, though, it seemed to resonate with his memory, even from the outside. All of the changes Isobel had made, the sachet smell and the feminine decoration, would never be able to erase the old man's presence again. Not for Rose.

The terrible truth she had learned while reading his journal had broken something in Rose's heart. But as she popped open her car door and stared up at the house, a bittersweet contentment touched her. Walt Hartung haunted this place. Maybe he always would. She'd feared that his secret would have forever tainted even the good memories she had of her grandfather, but found that was not the case.

"Rose," Mike said, as he climbed out of the car.

She glanced at him. His hand was still thickly bandaged, but somehow it didn't make him seem less capable. Mike had a rugged quality she'd not really noticed before. It stirred in his eyes, now.

"What the hell are we looking for, exactly?"

On the drive, she'd told him the whole story. To his credit, rather than start picking apart her theory, Mike had listened to all of the details and then begun to supply some of his own. By now, so many people had seen the hounds that their presence—and growing number—could not be denied. But he was aware of numerous incidents of bad luck and ominous coincidence that Rose had not heard about. Many people, it seemed, had also heard the eerie whistling sound that signified the presence of the hounds, and been unsettled by it.

It had filled her with relief to discover that she had an ally. Mike had given her hand a reassuring squeeze—the hand that wasn't on the steering wheel. In that moment, had she not been driving, she would have taken him in her arms. But such thoughts were for another day.

"Rose..." he prodded.

"I honestly don't know. I guess we'll know when we find it," she said as they sprinted for the front steps, well aware that her grandmother could not be far behind them.

She used her key to open the door. The hardwood in the foyer creaked underfoot as she stepped inside and turned on the lights. Mike followed her in and Rose slammed the door and locked it behind her.

"Some kind of container? Like a jar or something?" he asked.

She shrugged, glancing around, surveying the immaculate living room and the hallway ahead. What could she say?

"I don't think we can assume that. It isn't water, or his ashes, or something. This is all mystic bullshit to me, but my guess? It'll be something important to him, or to her."

Rose gnawed her lip for a few seconds. If her grandmother really loved him—and no matter what a bitch she'd been, it seemed she had—then Isobel wouldn't have imbued the old man's spiritual essence in something that only had significance for her.

"Scratch that. Something *he* cared about. I mean, I don't know for sure. Could be the toilet plunger or the cookie jar. But we don't have any way to tell. What we need is to find something she's got hidden. So we look everywhere an old woman would hide things. Kitchen cabinets, bathroom vanities, bedroom drawers, closets, under the bed."

She rattled all of that off even as she started into the kitchen. Mike followed her, but kept going toward the stairs and then vaulted up them two and three at a time.

Rose glanced around the kitchen, with its muted floral pattern walls and sensible clock on the wall. Nothing odd or interesting for her grandmother. She crouched down in front of the cabinet where the pots and pans were kept, yanked the doors open, and started pulling everything out with a clatter, upending the bigger pots to make sure nothing would fall out.

Not here, she thought as she stood and glanced around. It wouldn't be here. She didn't know why she'd even considered it. It would be something personal, and her grandmother would have kept it close by. Rose had watched too much television. This wasn't some drug dealer's house, where she might find a plastic packet taped to the inside of the toilet tank or wrapped up in the freezer.

"Stupid," she muttered to herself.

The clock ticked.

Rose raced out of the kitchen. As she reached the corridor she heard a car door slam outside. Isobel had arrived.

"Damn it."

She hit the stairs at a run and called out to Mike as she went up. Her shoulder grazed a framed picture on the wall and she twisted around just in time to see it fall—a photo of Rose herself with her grandparents, in a time before Walt Hartung's mind had begun to deteriorate. The glass shattered when the frame struck the stairs.

When Rose looked up, Mike had appeared at the landing above her.

"Anything?" she asked as she reached him.

More framed photographs hung on the walls in the little hall on the landing. A spider plant dangled over the edges of a vaguely Asian looking stand in a corner. There were four doors up here—master bedroom, guest bedroom, bathroom, and what had once been Grandad's study and was now Isobel's sewing room.

"Looked under the bathroom sink, under the bed and in the closet in the guest room. Just started with the sewing stuff—"

From downstairs came the muffled sound of the front door being unlocked. Mike shot Rose a look and she nodded. Then she pointed toward the sewing room, gesturing for him to get back to it, and she bolted into her grandparents' bedroom.

The smell struck her first. Perfume and baby powder. The room had always been immaculate, even before her grandfather had gone into the nursing home. But now it had a Spartan quality that seemed new to her. Elegant bedspread, cozy rocking chair, lamps, and a bureau with a tall mirror behind it and various items spread over its surface with precision. Hand-blown glass perfume bottle, antique hand mirror and brush, a small frame containing the young Walt and Isobel in their wedding photo, and a hand-carved box of dark wood that had sat there for as long as Rose could remember.

From downstairs, her grandmother called her name, the weight of sorrow in the old woman's voice. A creak on the stairs announced that she had started up toward the second floor.

Rose dropped to her knees and looked under the bed. She yanked open the nightstand drawer and fished through foot creams and Vicks bottles, a rosary, and costume jewelry her grandmother wouldn't dream of mixing with the real stuff in her jewelry box. Isobel called out to her again. Rose could hear Mike clattering around in the sewing room, tossing things aside. On instinct, she wanted to shout at him to stop, hating the sound of such haphazard ruin. But the stakes were too high for sentiment.

"Shit," she whispered.

"Rose!" her grandmother shouted, from the top of the stairs. "Please, stop."

She spun, scanning the room, and her gaze fell upon the bureau again, and the carved box that sat there. It had always been there, and so she'd barely recognized its presence. In the back of her mind, she felt sure she must once have known what lay within it, but could not remember.

The swish of her grandmother's mourning dress approached from the corridor. Rose rushed to the bureau and picked up the box. The moment she opened it, the breath rushed from her lungs. Inside lay a blue-striped ribbon with a medal on the end—her grandfather's Navy Distinguished Service Medal. Why hadn't this been in the nursing home with him? Rose held the open box in one hand and brushed her fingers across the medal. A shudder went through her, and the room seemed to grow colder.

"Don't you touch that. Don't you dare."

Rose turned, breath coming in tiny, shallow gasps. Her grandmother stood in the doorway, lips pressed tightly together, tears upon her cheeks. Behind the old woman, Mike stood in the corridor, coiled with tension. He didn't know what to do, whether he should interfere. Rose understood.

"Put it back, Rose."

Swallowing, she shook her head.

"Goddamn you, girl," her grandmother said, eyes narrowed with grief and desperation. "Put it back."

Rose held the open box in her hand. It felt strangely heavy.

"You can't save him," she told her grandmother. "What's done...it was done a long time ago. All you're going to do is kill the rest of us, and then they'll come and take him, but we'll all be dead. Do you really think that's what he'd want?"

Isobel pursed her lips. "Did you ever love him?"

Rose shook her head in disgust. "More than you can imagine. And if *you* loved him as much as you claim, you won't do this in his memory."

Mike shifted in the corridor. The old woman took a step into the room and he followed, on edge, ready to act if it became necessary. Rose saw self-loathing in his eyes, a kind man hating himself for what he might be forced to do.

"You don't understand. You couldn't. For years, he told me about the hounds. He saw them every few months, one or two of them pacing his car or watching him through a window, following him in the woods. All along he told me they'd come for him in the end. And I didn't believe him. Do you understand that? I didn't believe him!

"Not until the first time I saw them. Those eyes, shining in the dark, and the quiet size of the things—I knew right off they weren't just dogs. Then I knew that he'd been telling the truth all along."

Rose felt anger rising in her. Her face flushed. "You knew what he'd done. You were supposed to be with Davey and you knew that Grandad had let him die, and you just forgave him!"

The old woman's eyes darkened. "You don't think before you speak, Rose. You never did. Your grandfather didn't kill David, but I wish he had. He'd talk of love with his fists, that one. When he shipped out, I prayed, but not like the other girls whose beaus were going to sea. I prayed Davey would never come back. Your grandfather made a terrible mistake, and it weighed on him. But I looked at him, and I saw my savior."

Rose stared at her. "Even so, what he did...it wasn't right. He didn't know he was protecting you. He was protecting himself."

All trace of emotion—even grief—vanished from Isobel's face and she stepped forward, thrusting out her hand.

"Give it to me."

"No." Rose shook her head and took a step back. "I don't know how you did this, how you could know how to do it, but I'm putting an end to it."

Trembling with fury, her grandmother started toward her. Mike stepped up behind her and put his good hand on her shoulder, startling her. Isobel spun on him.

"Get your hands off of me. Who do you think you are?"

"Just a guy who doesn't want the world to end because of the selfishness of one old man," Mike replied.

Isobel ignored him. "I went through hell for him, Rose. I lived with his terror. And I loved him in spite of it. He'd saved me, and I wanted to save him in return. For years, I searched for some kind of magic to keep his spirit safe. I'd never believed in such things, but seeing the hellhounds again and again, how could I not believe?

"I studied legends and I talked to people who had faith in them, and in witchcraft. In Montreal, I met a woman who showed me what to do, how to catch his spirit in that box, trap it with his medal."

Her emotionless mask shattered. Isobel twisted in anguish as every wretched shred of her grief revealed itself upon her face.

"Don't you understand how much it hurt me, to do that? Can you even begin to imagine how dreadful a thing it was to have to do? But it was better than the alternative, Rose. If you do this, if you give him to the hounds, he'll suffer forever. The devil takes his own, Rose! The devil takes his own."

Rose felt heat on her cheeks, tasted salt on her lips, and realized that she had also begun to cry.

"Grandad could have come forward at any time," she said, voice quavering, hands shaking. "No matter what Davey'd done to you, he didn't know that, did he? All he wanted was to save his own skin, and he let his best friend be executed in his place. Even after, when Davey was dead, he could have taken the consequences for what he'd done. But he never did."

A sob escaped her lips. Mike stared at her and she could see he wanted to come to her, but Rose shook her head and took a deep breath, taking control of herself.

"It's killing a part of me," she told her grandmother. "But I won't let the world pay for what he did."

Rose snapped the medal box shut, and started for the door.

"No," her grandmother whispered, shaking her head. "No, Rose!"

The old woman reached for her. Mike tried gently to hold onto her arm, but Isobel shoved him away. Rose tried to pass her, but her grandmother grabbed hold of her, clawing at her, reaching for the box.

"Don't you do it! Please, stop!"

Rose held the box out of her reach and shook her grandmother off. Isobel had always been cold and distant with her. All her life, she had thought her grandmother was a selfish, callous woman with little love in her heart. Now she saw that she'd been wrong. Isobel Hartung could feel love, but it was all reserved for the man she'd always wanted, the man she'd forgiven for a heinous sin, because it served her own purposes.

Even so, Rose did not stop. The old woman's cries were torture, but there had never been any choice. She pulled away. Her grandmother tried to stop her. Mike slipped between them, grabbing Isobel's arms and holding her back as Rose went down the stairs. She cursed at him with shocking venom, vile profanity that Rose had never heard her grandmother utter before, and then crumbled to the ground and leaned herself against the wall, shuddering and weeping loudly.

Mike followed Rose downstairs.

She stood at the door with the box in one hand and the other on the knob. From outside, she could hear the high, keening sound that had so terrified her in the cemetery the other night.

The Whistlers had arrived.

—16—

Rose counted four of them at first.

The hell hounds stood arrayed across the front lawn of her grandparents' house, silently awaiting her. Mike could have stayed just inside the front door, but he remained at her side as she went out onto the steps. The eerie wail of the Whistlers had ceased, now, and though she could see the rise and fall of their massive chests—their black pelts gleaming in the moonlight—the hounds had fallen quiet.

One of the hounds had taken up a position on the roof of Rose's car. Its eyes shone in the dark, like those of its brothers. They were pinpoints of unnatural light, there in the shadows of the night.

Rose could not breathe. She wondered if they had been about to attack when she opened the door and interrupted them, or if they had somehow been waiting for her to emerge. And how had they found this place? Had their search finally borne terrible fruit, or had her discovery of the medal—of her grandfather's hidden soul—somehow drawn their attention?

It didn't matter. Nothing mattered, now, except the carved wooden box in her hand and what lay within it.

She went down the stairs and onto the front lawn. Mike followed, a step or two behind. She felt him freeze, and then he spoke her name in a whisper. Rose glanced at him, but he wasn't looking her way. She followed his gaze and saw two more of the sleek, enormous hounds slowly prowling toward them from around the side of the house.

"Six," she whispered. "There are six."

Her fingers clutched the wooden box so tightly that they hurt. Ice slid through her veins as she stared at the two approaching hounds, wondering what she would do if they charged. When they stopped twenty yards from her, Rose flinched. Mike brushed the back of his hand on her arm, and though it might have been accidental, she believed he had intended to make that small contact, just to reassure her that she wasn't alone.

"Put it down on the ground," he said, voice low and even. "Just set it down and we'll back away."

The words were eminently logical. Of course, that was what she had to do. Set down the box with her grandfather's war medal inside it, leave it there and just retreat into the house. Give the Whistlers what they came for, and all would be well.

She felt as though she were crumbling in upon herself. Grief welled up inside her and she lowered her head, clutching that carved box to her chest. Hot tears ran down her face, surprising her with their sudden arrival.

"Rose," Mike said.

The hell hound on top of her car leaped down from the roof, and the six of them took two steps nearer, tightening the half-circle they'd formed around the front door of the house. Rose and Mike were trapped there. The open door was their only retreat.

From inside came the sound of her grandmother, calling her name again, wracked with mournful sobs.

Rose tried to turn to Mike—tried to speak to him, to explain the crippling emotion sweeping through her—but she could not form words. Part of her hated her grandfather in that moment; hated him for having caused all of this with his cowardice and secrecy. Rose hated him because she had loved him so much.

Damn you, she thought, shaking her head, blinking away the tears.

The irony froze her.

Mike said her name again, gently urgent, and reached down to try to take the box from her hands. She pulled away from him. Her chest ached as though the hounds had already been at her, like they'd torn her open and ripped her heart out, and somehow she'd survived.

All the fear left her, replaced by a revulsion and despair unlike anything she could ever have imagined. The world of spirits and the justice of souls seemed so far beyond her. She was just a girl from Kingsbury who liked horses. Whatever her grandfather had done—sin or crime or shame—he could not possibly deserve whatever afterlife would be his once the Whistlers had collected him. Rose could not do it. She couldn't just give him over to damnation and torment.

Back in the house, her grandmother cried out to her again, as if she herself were haunting Rose from the spirit world.

Then, from somewhere to the east, over the tops of other houses and through acres of trees, came that high, keening whistle. Rose let out a shuddering breath, staring in the direction from which that eerie sound had come.

"There are six," Mike said, his voice terribly small.

But the hell hounds that encircled the front of her grandparents' house were silent and still, regarding them with gleaming eyes. Which meant that this sound, off in the distance but coming nearer, was the seventh.

"Rose," Mike prodded.

Her tears had gone cold upon her face, and she told herself it was the autumn breeze, not the chill inside her, that was responsible. A thousand moments played through her mind; holding her grandfather's hand while walking to the bakery, modeling her back-to-school clothes while he clapped in delight, the old songs he used to sing, a crackly-voiced Sinatra. Rose had loved the man for his wisdom and the way he had always been able to soothe her with gentle words and smiling eyes.

No matter what he had done, she would never be able to stop loving him for the role he had played in her life. She thought she could even forgive him for his cowardice—for letting another man die simply because he was too frightened to tell the truth—but she would never forget.

The distant, whistling cry drew nearer.

Mike must have said something further, urged her on. Her grandmother must have continued to call out to her. Rose could not hear either of them. The only sound that reached her was that eerie wail, like the screaming of the damned.

Her hands seemed to move of their accord. Mechanically, she flipped open the carved wooden box. The medal glinted within. A smell rose from the box, Old Spice and cinnamon, and for a second it felt to her as though her grandfather was right there with her, standing beside her in the darkness.

Rose felt the weight of the moment, more powerful even than her grief. She took the medal from the box and tossed it onto the lawn. The hounds did not move. In her mind's eyes, she'd pictured them leaping at it, tearing at it, even fighting over it, but they remained completely still. Rose felt the damp streaks drying on her face. There would be no more tears for her. Her chest rose and fell with her breathing, as though she mirrored the Whistlers themselves.

The last of the Whistlers howled again, oh so very close, now.

"Jesus, Rose," Mike rasped.

She dropped the wooden box. He slipped his fingers into hers and they clasped hands. Rose squeezed his hand tightly.

"Take it, you evil fuckers!" she screamed at the hounds. "Just take it and go!"

As if they'd been awaiting her permission, one of the hounds trotted forward, bent its snout to the ground, and snatched up the medal. They seemed, in that moment, as docile as lap dogs. But they were too silent to be ordinary animals, too monstrous to be dogs, too sleek and ominous to be anything of this world.

One by one, they turned and slipped away. Rose and Mike stood hand in hand and watched them vanish into the night, black wraiths lost in shadow, and she knew that they carried a part of her away with them forever, a piece of that little girl who had once thought her grandfather the greatest man ever to walk the earth.

The carved, wooden box that had sat for decades atop the bureau in her grandparents' room lay on the grass at her feet, empty.

—17—

The morning of Walter Hartung's funeral, the sun shone brightly down upon those who had gathered in their grief to pay their last respects. Whenever a breeze kicked up, sending brown and orange leaves skittering across the cemetery and piling them up against tombstones, a chilly hint of winter could be felt. But otherwise, the blue sky and warm sunshine conspired in a masquerade, a pretense that autumn had not yet arrived.

Even the day was a lie.

Early that morning, Rose had argued with her mother—loudly, and perhaps irreparably. Though she would not speak to her parents about the events of the past few days, aware that it would be impossible to convince them of the truth, she was determined not to stand with her grandmother during the church service, or at the burial. Both her mother and father had attempted to get to the bottom of her refusal, and then resorted to attempts to make her feel guilty about it. With regret, if only because she did not want to hurt her mother, who had after all lost her father, she had stood her ground.

In the front row of mourners, on that beautiful day, with the sun warming them, her parents flanked her grandmother. Rose noticed that neither of them touched her; not so much as a gentle, reassuring hand. Isobel Hartung had never been the sort of woman who invited human contact. That had not changed.

Rose stood two rows back with Alan and Jenny on her left and Mike on her right. He still held her hand. The previous night, when the hounds had all gone, she had driven him back to the funeral home to retrieve his car. There had been a moment, dropping him off, when she thought he might try to kiss her and had been torn by her desire to feel that intimacy and the knowledge that if he had done it under those circumstances, anything that might develop between them would be forever tied to that night.

Mike had not kissed her.

But this morning, holding his hand, Rose liked his firm grip and the silent strength he lent her with his touch. Last night, she'd had very little sleep. She had never felt so lonely, so isolated, and the memory of his hand in hers had lingered, helping her make it through until dawn. When she'd woken, she'd almost expected him to be there in bed with her.

She had no idea what the future might hold for them, but for now, she was grateful for the comfort of his touch. Jenny and Alan lent their support as well. Jenny glanced at Rose every few minutes, and eventually linked arms with her, as though at any moment they might dance off along the yellow brick road. The gesture lightened Rose's heart, just for a moment, but that was enough.

As for tears, however, this morning Rose had none. All her crying had been done the night before. Her last goodbye had taken place on the front lawn of her grandparents' house, staring into the night. The funeral service felt almost like an afterthought.

Her grandmother and her parents obviously did not agree. Whatever injury she'd done them by not standing with them at the graveside, she added insult to it through her inability to summon tears. Rose felt strangely numb to this knowledge. Many in the crowd had been at the wake the night before and witnessed her departure—followed swiftly by her grandmother's—and those who had not been in attendance had surely heard rumor of it by now. Rose's refusal to stand with her grandmother only reinforced the awkwardness that already existed.

The priest had his say, dust to dust, and all of that. Rose tuned him out. She knew the true fate of the man they were lowering into the ground, and she could not stand to listen. The sun made her sleepy. A chilly wind danced around her legs, swirling leaves past her and fluttering the hem of her long, black coat.

"You'll get through this," Mike whispered to her.

She nodded. That much was true. A man had died, but men died every day. Rose and the other people she loved were still breathing. Her friends had gathered protectively around her. One death, one funeral, wasn't the end of the world.

Not this time.

When the graveside service had come to an end, the priest beckoned for her grandmother to take a flower and throw it on top of the coffin, a gesture of farewell. Rose stared at the porcelain-masked old woman, waiting for Isobel to look up at her. But her grandmother never did look up. She behaved as though entirely unaware of Rose's presence, or even her existence.

Rose found she could not bring herself to care. But when her mother dropped a flower on Grandad's casket, weeping, and shot her a look of confusion and sorrow, she felt her heart go cold. Rose had done nothing wrong, but her grandfather's sins had cost her a great deal.

Still, when it came her turn to drop a flower on his casket, she prayed for the old man's soul, though she already knew the answer.

When the mourners began to disperse—black and gray figures under a gloriously blue sky, walking back to their cars across rustling beds of crisp autumn leaves—Rose paused a moment to watch her grandmother and her parents climb into the limousine that had brought them there. Those who had troubled themselves to come out this morning would be invited back to that strangely empty house to reminisce about the one who had died, who they thought had gone on before them to whatever awaited them all.

Rose and her friends drove to the Pennywhistle instead, and raised a single toast to Walt Hartung, not for his sins but in spite of them.

In February, on a day as bitter and cold as Isobel Hartung's heart, Rose returned to the cemetery to listen to the same priest utter the same hollow assurances and remembrances. Most of the mourners were the same, but the crowd was smaller. Whether this could be attributed to the harsh winter weather or to the simple fact that fewer people had liked her grandmother enough to be bothered showing up, Rose couldn't have said, and wouldn't hazard a guess.

Isobel had followed her spouse to the grave the way that so many men and women do, after a certain age.

Once again, Rose did not stand with her family at the graveside. Her mother had forbidden her to do so, but she would have refused in any case. Instead, she stood four rows back on the frozen, snow-covered ground, accompanied by her closest friends. Mike had his arm around her, and she huddled against him for protection against the wind, and against the winter that sometimes encroached upon the human heart.

Rose did not pray for her grandmother. She only stood and scanned the February shadows cast by crypts and headstones, and the trees that encircled the cemetery, searching for dark, silent figures that did not belong, and listening for their telltale whistle.